Praise for

IN ANOTHER PLACE, NOT HERE

"Startling, as if we had entered the
heart of another human being."
— *Books in Canada*

"This is simply a stunning book."
— *The Globe and Mail*

"A sensuous, lyrical work of fiction
in the tradition of... Toni Morrison."
— *The Toronto Star*

"... breathtakingly beautiful language....
Brand's prose takes up residence on your tongue,
demanding to be read and spoken aloud."
— *The Financial Post*

"A beautiful book that moves the reader with its evocative
language, often closer to poetry than prose, and its insights into
the immigrant experience of Caribbean women."
— *The Montreal Gazette*

"With this book, this marvellous love letter,
Brand emerges as a writer of the first rank....
This book is one of the classics of our culture."
— *The Halifax Chronicle-Herald*

"Brand's style intoxicates.... [She] is one of the freshest, fiercest voices in Canadian letters...There are dizzying, intoxicating verbal acrobatics on almost every page, passages of painfully lyric beauty."
— *The Edmonton Journal*

"Luscious...as sensuous as the smooth coral pulp of mangoes."
— *The Ottawa Citizen*

"Brand's mesmerizing voice lures the reader through a plot that oscillates between past and present. Her rendering of the island's slave history is sublimely evocative.... The novel reinforces Brand's status as a significant voice for the Caribbean-Canadian experience."
— *Maclean's*

"The novel is very much a poet's novel, with strong, lyrical evocation of passions, moods and places, skillfully blending reality and fantasy"
— *Calgary Herald*

"Remarkable...What Brand unfolds in this novel... is a profound understanding of two women.... As readers, we enter a vision of the world that is fully and powerfully realized.... Erotic passages are stunning.... At the end...it's virtually impossible to resist the urge to return to the beginning."
— *Xtra!*

"The remarkable poet Dionne Brand now gives us a fierce, sensuous novel of women in migration, political and emotional. Concrete and visionary as a dream, relentless as the history it reveals, *In Another Place, Not Here* is a work of great beauty and moral imagination."
— Adrienne Rich

IN ANOTHER PLACE, NOT HERE

DIONNE BRAND

VINTAGE CANADA
A Division of Random House of Canada

FIRST VINTAGE CANADA EDITION, 1997

Copyright © 1996 by Dionne Brand

Published in Canada by Vintage Canada,
a division of Random House of Canada Limited,
Toronto, in 1997. Originally published in Canada by
Alfred A. Knopf Canada, Toronto, in 1996. Distributed
by Random House of Canada Limited, Toronto.

Canadian Cataloguing in Publication Data

Brand, Dionne
In another place, not here

ISBN 0-394-28179-9

I. Title.

PS8553.R27515 1997   C813'.54   C95-932297-3

PR9199.3.B715 1997

printed and bound in Canada

10 9 8 7 6 5 4 3

to my aunts Phyllis and Joan —
to their big hands,
to their bigger laughter

Elizete, beckoned

[handwritten annotations:]

use of imagery:
→ figurative language
→ female narrative

oppressive labor

Romantic ♡ story - does NOT dominate
→ resist traditional patriacrical practises.
→ fundamental material struggles
→ work/political struggle.

attached to religion — mercy
"by the Grace of God"
— descriptor of her lover.
→ power/substance/meaning

[left margin, vertical:] labor/exhaustion → women is grace

GRACE. IS GRACE, YES. And I take it, quiet, quiet, like thiefing sugar. From the word she speak to me and the sweat running down she in that sun, one afternoon as I look up saying to myself, how many more days these poor feet of mine can take this field, these blades of cane like razor, this sun like coal pot. Long as you have to eat, girl. I look up. That woman like a drink of cool water. The four o'clock light thinning she dress, she back good and strong, the sweat raining off in that moment when I look and she snap she head around, that wide mouth blowing a wave of tiredness away, pulling in one big breath of air, them big white teeth, she, falling to the work again, she, falling into the four o'clock sunlight. I see she. Hot, cool and wet. I sink the machete in my foot, careless, blood blooming in the stalks of cane, a sweet ripe smell wash me

[handwritten annotations at bottom:]
finds her work attractive
Not the norm
female physical strength ⟹ POWER

(girls glow don't sweat!)

3

repetition of "s"

Eliete pays a
price for her vision
→ grounding the [?]stor[?]
→ work demands full attr
→ dominates

faint. With pain. Wash the field, spinning green mile after green mile around she. See she sweat, sweet like sugar.

Romance
Pleasure
Work
Pain.

I never wanted nothing big from the world. Who is me to want anything big or small. Who is me to think I is something. I born to clean Isaiah' house and work cane since I was a child and say what you want Isaiah feed me and all I have to do is lay down under him in the night and work the cane in the day. It have plenty woman waiting their whole blessed life for that and what make me turn woman and leave it I don't know, but it come. Bad spirit they say, bad spirit or blessed, it come, what make me notice Verlia' face spraying sweat in the four o'clock heat.

Circular narrative

Because you see I know I was going to lose something, because Verl was surer than anything I see before, surer than the day I get born, because nothing ever happen to me until Verl come along and when Verl come along I see my chance out of what ordinary, out of the plenty day when all it have for a woman to do is lie down and let a man beat against she body, and work cane and chop up she foot and make children and choke on the dryness in she chest and have only one road in and the same road out and know that she tied to the ground and can never lift up. And it wasn't nothing Verl do or say or even what Verl was or what Verl wanted because even now I can't swear but is just that I see Verl coming, like a shower of rain coming that could just wash me cool and that was sufficient and if God spite me for this, is so things is.

There is another world out there, verlia shows her this.

opens up new
potentials.

I abandon everything for Verlia. I sink in Verlia and let she flesh swallow me up. I devour she. <u>She open me up like any morning.</u> Limp, limp and rain light, soft to the marrow. She make me wet. She tongue scorching like hot sun. I love that shudder between her legs, love the plain wash and sea of her, the swell and bloom of her softness. And is all. And if is all I could do on the earth, is all.

She would say, "Open your eyes, I want to see what you're feeling." I don't know what she see in my eyes but she stare into me until I break. Her look say, "Elizete, you is bigger than me by millennia and you can hold me between your legs like rock hold water. You are wearing me away like years and I wonder if you can see me beyond rock and beyond water as something human that need to eat and can die, even as you dive into me today like a fish and want nothing or so you say." Something say to me, Elizete, you is not big enough for nothing you done live and V<u>erlia is your grace.</u>

reasons
why /how

Isaiah gone mad catching me lying underneath Verlia, and even the sure killing in him couldn't sweep me away from the sweetness of her. I didn't even raise my head. I finished loving Verlia taking she face and she skin black as water in my hand so I was to remember what I lose something for. I never see him after that. They say he sit under a fishing net in Las Cuevas now and he talk to himself, they say he don't remember me but call out the name of the Venezuelan woman what first was his wife and what make

struggle → female wins.
Power of women → drives him to
insanity.

DIONNE BRAND

him carry she fishing one night and when day break she was not there. They say he is like a jumbie, and is best for me and he to leave that way for it have too much between we, and is vindication what make him open the door. Isaiah was a hard man, a hard man down to his skin. Is best I didn't kill him as I plan, is best I didn't pour the milk of buttercups in his eyes and blind him, is best I didn't sling his neck off, is best I didn't rub his head with killing root. Is best I see this woman when I raise up in my swing, when the sweat was falling like rain from she. I say is grace the way it happen and is grace. ~~force above her~~ → prevents her from killing Isaiah

He and me story done right there, one time. It have nothing to say else about it. overcome male oppression

Everything make sense from then the way flesh make sense settling into blood. I think to myself how I must be was sleeping all this time. I must be was in a trance because it was as if Verl wake me up to say, "Girl, put on your clothes. Let we go now." It have ways of trancing people and turning them against they very self and I suspect Isaiah now with his prayer book and his plait hair but I have no time with him. I suspect the woman I grow with and she hands that can't stop growing things. I suspect the cane. I suspect Moriah. I suspect my life. I suspect the moon. Everything. What don't meet you don't pass you.

Verl was sure. Sure of everything. And sure like that was not something in my life. I was sure that I would wake up

A womens story

each day, I was sure that I had to work cane, I was sure that the man they give me to was Isaiah Ferdinand. I was sure that he would illtreat me. I was sure that each night I would dream of miles of cane waving. Things like this. I was sure iguana would be thirsty enough to cross the road if the dry season was too long, I was sure birds would fly across the house in the morning. I was sure of what anybody would be sure of. Spite, hunger, rain. But Verl is sure of what she make in her own mind and what she make didn't always exist.

I like it how she leap. Run in the air without moving. I watch she make she way around we as if she was from here, all the time moving faster than the last thing she say. It come so I know where she standing in the field without looking for she. Because she moving, moving, moving all the time without moving. If I didn't like it she would frighten me.

There is a heat that looks like glass waving if you make your eyes look far. Everybody didn't like that moving but everybody eyes was on she the first time she come. She was walking in that heat and we was all in the shed eating. Some was laying down for the while and she reach and start busy busy giving out papers. She look like the transport drop she by the junction and she walk in. People get up and start going but the old ones listen to she. I know why they listen. Is not often that some young one with soft hands and skin smelling of the kind of sweat they make in the town come talking to them. They touch up she clothes and she hands and she face and say "Who child is you?" They play with she and kiss she up. And it give them a softness like how they might have been if they live in town and if they had money and if their life was different. They give she water and they give she fry fish. They tell she don't drink fast. They love it when she just eat as if she don't scorn them but they laugh when she say what she want. They laugh long. And then they hush.

Nobody here can remember when they wasn't here. I come here with Isaiah. He show me the room and he show me the washtub and he show me the fire and he show me the road. He tell me never let him catch me at the junction. I didn't believe him but I find out soon when I catch the end of his whip. That was long time now. No need to remember. I don't even remember when I stop trying to run away, stop trying to make that junction. It was long. He would always be at that junction when I get there. I tried for a long time. I think to myself one day he is going to miss, one day. One day when he think I train, he is going to miss. But I stop. He get his way. When I see that it was his play, I resign. He stop watching me but then I could not remember why I was trying to get there. Didn't have no place to go anyway when I think of it. Trying to get to the junction so much I forget where I was going. I know every track leading to it but when I get there and see Isaiah, it come like he was the end of it. I used to have some place in mind I know but... One time,

I plotting my way through the mangle, one of these old ones I never expect ask me "Where you running running so all the time?" The spite of the thing hit me and it take me by surprise, and I suppose I didn't have nowhere in mind except not here. Cold water just run in my feet then. You trust old people to know better. Why they wouldn't want good for me? If you can't see a way for yourself, see it for somebody else nah? So all of that is how I wear away.

Not a bone in she like that. Verlia. Hatred and anger, but not spite. Spite is loving to see people suffer. She say to me that you could get used to suffering. She say is what curve we back to the cane. Is all we know. Hatred you could out and out deal with, and anger, but not spite. It was her speed though, the way she could make the junction still standing in front of you, the way she could move fast in she head. People say this is not people to trust, people who know what you saying before you say it, people hurrying you up to move, them kinda people busy busy going someplace soon but I was ready for Verlia. She get send for me.

She was burning. You could see she burning bright. Before you know it they making sweet bread for she, before you know it washtub full of ice cream done plan. Before you know it she invite for Sunday. I suppose not only me see rescue when she reach.

I used to wonder who she went home to; watch she walk to the junction in the evening half dead and wonder if her quickness fall away on the transport, wondered if she was the same in town, what she kitchen smell like, and if she plant okra and what she think. Soon I was only wondering about she. I watch she disappear up the junction and I wait for she to break it in the mornings. Is nothing that draw me to she but that and the way she want nothing from me and the way she brand new and come from another life.

After the woman I lived with die on me I was given to Isaiah. She passed on when I was not yet a young lady. It seem to me that one day I wake up under Isaiah. Isaiah ride me every night. I was a horse for his jumbie. His face was like the dead over me on the floor when he cry out for the woman who leave him as he ride me to hell. Each night I hear him say these words as if I should pity him. "When I meet that Venezuelan woman it was the last day of my life. She sail me like a ship. That woman could tell stories. It was through one of her tales that I arrived at this sandpit with my back breaking and my eyes burning with this sweat, with her fine clothes and her fine ideas; I laid every brick on that stone house where she take man in front of me. My hair turn red and I never scream in this place yet." With that he ride me again. These times I wander, I turn my head to the wall and travel in the dust tunnels of wood lice. I cover my self in their fine, fine sand, I slide through the tunnel and I see all where I have to go, and I try to reach where they live and I

try to be like them because try as I did when I was little I
never see one of them yet only the rifts on the walls. Is so
they work in secret and in their own company. Is so I travel
the walls of this room catching hell and Isaiah' advantage till
morning. I dream every day to break a shovel over his head
which he plait in braids for he read in the Bible that he
should not cut his hair. Every evening when they was in season he would climb the land above the quarry to pick cashew
fruit and nuts. I would stand at the bottom looking at him
hoping that the bitter juice from the fruit burn him to death
for I know that it is poison. I carried a mountain inside of
me. The thought of him and his hardness cut at the red
stone in me from sun-up to sundown. I went in the evenings
after work to the sand quarry while he sleep. The salmon
dank sides rise up around me and I was silent there. It was a
place where I had peace, or I wouldn't call it peace but calm,
and I shovelled, the sweat drizzling from my body as I think
and think of escaping him. I did not sympathize with him,
no matter what he said that red woman do to him. What she
make him eat, how she tie his mind. It could not compen-
sate for what he do to me. There in the damp, it make me
calm, calm, calm and hollow inside me. If I dig enough it
cool me and take my mind off the junction. I feel my body
full up and burst. All my skin split. Until I was so tired I
could not run. I dream of running though, to Aruba or
Maracaibo. I hear about these place. Yes, Maracaibo. I love

[handwritten left margin: knowledge of plants / animals]

[handwritten bottom: dream of running]
[handwritten: dreams => own desires are revealed oppressed in real world not in conscience world]

the sound of it yet I have never seen it. I dream of taking his neck with a cutlass and running to Maracaibo, yes. I imagine it as a place with thick and dense vine and alive like veins under my feet. I dream the vine, green and plump, blood running through it and me too running running, spilling blood. Vine like rope under my feet, vine strapping my legs and opening when I walk. Is like nowhere else. I destroying anything in my way. I want it to be peaceful there. The air behind me close thick as mist whenever I move and Maracaibo open rough and green and dense again. I dream I spit milk each time my mouth open. My stomach will swell and vines will burst out. I dream it is a place where a woman can live after she done take the neck of a man. Fearless. I dream my eyes, black and steady in my black face and never close. I will wear a black skirt, shapely like a wing and down to my toes. I will fly to Maracaibo in it and you will see nothing of me but my black eyes in my black face and my black skirt swirling over thick living vine. I dream of flying in my skirt to Maracaibo. I want to go to Maracaibo if it is the last thing I do. This black skirt will melt like soot if it get touched. And my face too. One day I will do it, for Isaiah don't know my mind in this. He too busy in his own mind now. He make his heart too hard to know anyone else. One day I will done calculate him.

The time in between as I say I don't remember but it must have been there because by the time I recognize myself

I was a big woman and the devil was riding me. How I reach here is one skill I learn hard. The skill of forgetfulness. So I shovel in this pit from morning till night, cut cane when it in season and lie under this man at night until one day I see this woman talking, talking like she know what she is saying and everybody around listening. I walk past because I have no time for no woman talking. It don't mean nothing. It don't matter what woman say in the world, take it from me. This woman with her mouth flying…cheups. I hear something about co-operative. Black people could ever co-operate? This little girl too fast again. Her mouth too fast, she tongue flying ahead of sheself. Face plain as day, mouth like a ripe mango and teeth, teeth like a horse. I en't talk to she then. They tell me she is for the revo, that she is for taking all the land and giving it to people who work it all their life. Revolution, my ass. Let foolish old people believe she. Is only them have time to sit down and get wrap up in her mouth and think Oliviere and them will let go any land. Is only one thing will fix Oliviere and them and is the devil because them is the devil' son self. I pass by her going my way and didn't that woman skin she big teeth for me and look at me so clear is as if she see all my mind clear through to Maracaibo. Her look say, "I know you. I know you plan to sling off a man' neck and go to Maracaibo." I brazen she look and I pass she straight. Smelling vetiver and salt, fresh ironed clothes I pass she. Nobody from no town coming to look me in my face so. Nobody coming here to tell me what I done know. Anything she do could help me? Who she think she is come preaching here? Revolution, my backside. Then, she say "Sister." And I could not tell if it was a breeze passing in that heat-still day or if I hear the word. "Sister." I know I hear it, murmuring just enough to seem as if it was said but not something that only have sense in saying. I know I hear it silver, silver clinking like bracelets when a woman lift her arm to comb hair. Silvery, silvery the wind take it. It hum low and touch everything on the road. Things in me. I feel it cuff my back. I have to take air. A spirit in the road. It make a silence. It feel like rum going through my throat, warm and violent so the breath of her mouth brush my ear. Sweet sweet, my tongue sweet to answer she and it surprise me how I want to touch she teeth and hold she mouth on that word. I keep walking. I don't answer. But I regret every minute until I see she next.

The next time she come playing she trying to swing cutlass with she mouth moving as fast as you please about strike. Strike and demand a share in the estate. Well, look at bold face. We navel string bury here, she say, and we mother and we father and everybody before them. Oliviere use it up like manure for the cane, and what we get, one barrack room and credit in he store until we owe he more than he owe we, and is thief he thief this place in the first place. The people listen to she and smile because they know she make sense but she don't know what a hard people these Oliviere is. Is not just people navel string bury here is their shame and their body. They churn that up in the soil here too. It have people they just shoot and leave for corbeau to eat them. What left make the cane fat and juicy. She come from town and God knows where light, light and easy so. She not ready yet. One for she, she work hard. She body en't make for this, well who body make for it, but she do it.

She break my swing. It was the quiet. When I get used to she talking as I bend into the cane, when I done add she up for the swing so I wouldn't miss doing how much I need to do to make the quota, when I make she voice count in the stroke, I don't hear she no more. I swing up. What she doing now, like she tired talk at last. Good Lord! I say to myself, God wasn't joking when he make you girl. She was in front of me, staring my way, sweating as if she come out of a river. She was brilliant. I could see she head running ahead of we, she eyes done cut all the cane, she is not here, she dreaming of things we don't dream. I wanted to touch the shine of her, to dry off she whole body and say "Don't work it so hard," show she how to swing, how to tie up she waist so that she back would last, shield she legs so that the sheaf wouldn't cut. That is the first time I feel like licking she neck. She looked like the young in me, the not beaten down and bruised, the not pounded between my legs, the not lost my mother, the not raped, the not blooded, the not tired. She looked like me fresh, fresh, searching for good luck tea, leave my house broom, come by here weed. It ease me. It sweet sweet. A woman can be a bridge, limber and living, breathless, because she don't know where the bridge might lead, she don't need no assurance except that it would lead out with certainty, no assurance except the arch and disappearance. At the end it might be the uptake of air, the chasm of what she don't know, the sweep and soar of sheself unhandled, making sheself a way to cross over. A woman can be a bridge from these bodies whipping cane. A way to cross over. I see in she face how she believe. She glance quick as if unimportant things was in she way, like Oliviere, like fright. She eyes move as if she was busy going somewhere, busy seeing something and all this cane all this whipping and lashing was a hindrance. Then like a purposeful accident she eyes rest on me, and she face open, them big teeth push out to laugh for me, sweat flying, she fall again to the cutlass.

Under the samaan tree is where I grow up. It was wide and high and the light between what it leave of the sky was soft and it look like a woman with hands in the air. A samaan is a tree with majesty and I think of this samaan as my mother. She wave from far and the sun pass through she, and she was my keeper. Until the woman I was given to come home from the field the samaan was my mother. I wait there whole day under the tree and I play in the dirt. When I was big enough to boil water and not catch the house on fire, the woman they give me to make me keep the house and bring she food to the field. And after that I work with she in the garden. First I pull weed, then I dig dasheen, then I learn all the plants there and on the hillside though I don't know their names. But I know which grass bitter and which one good for fever. Why I don't know their names is because the woman they give me to don't know their names, and she don't know them because she ma before and her ma before that as far as she know didn't know neither but it's for a reason which she tell me.

She say when she great-great-great-ma come here she was grieving bad for where she come from. And when she done calculate the heart of this place, that it could not yield to her grief, she decide that this place was not nowhere and is so she call it. Nowhere. She say nothing here have no name. She never name none of her children, nor the man she had was to sleep with and she never answer to the name that they give she which was Adela. After all that they say she kill the man that buy she and keep she in that place, for she look him full in his face until he dead. Up here in the valley, when she reach for the first time, was the estate of one Oliviere many times this one father. Every evening when she come home from the cocoa fields, as was cocoa they mind then, she make sure and pass by the big house and she draw a circle in the ground and sprinkle one stone in it that was her eye and spit the man name, with blood from biting she mouth, into the centre. Rain or sun she do it for three years. And finally one day he drop dead on that very spot. They say she could work good obeah but she say is not obeah what kill him, is his own wicked mind what make him die in his wicked name. She had spit all his evil into that circle and he could not resist himself. They say she curse him and all his generations into perpetuity. Just so she say it, yes, and that they should not be rescued not even if she get back to where she come from, which she surely was going to do when she dead. Even now, long since she gone, all how they

Religion / magic developed in new world

Power of the curse evoking power of language

strength of women kind
— despite size
IN ANOTHER PLACE, NOT HERE
Positive qualities→determination/ patients

prosper, their soul damn to hell and none of them is ever happy with life. She was a small woman they say, not any kind of woman you would think was dangerous but the day she make she mind determine all her desire come to one purpose. Yet and after all she did not learn the grace of drying up her womb even after eight children. She spill and spill so and she mothered not a one. She only see their face as bad luck and grudge them the milk from her breast. She eat paw-paw seed until it make them sick in she womb. The charm she tried to use against each one was left half done in them so, till all of she generations have a way so that nothing is right with them neither. Bad mind and goat mouth follow them and discomfort so that none of them sleep, each have some affliction. She tied the charm around her waist in pouches of dust on a string so tight she skin bleed and grow over them and she forget them. Adela call this place Nowhere and with that none of the things she look at she take note of or remember or pass on. She insist so much is nowhere she gone blind with not seeing. Cause sheself blindness, yes. A caul draw over her eyes. Whatever they bless on she curse. And that was she inheritance. And that is how I don't know the names of things though I know their face. I know there is names for things but I can not be sure of the truth of them.

I ask the woman I living with when we will know the names of things and if Adela reach home yet and if she will

19

send them give we. For is home Adela say she was going when she dead, seeing as how she couldn't make it there alive. Adela is dead now long gone. I think about her when I get to know about her. I watch things and I wonder what Adela would call this if it wasn't nowhere, pull and throw bush, make haste weed, jump up and kiss me flowers, waste of time plant, red berry poison, beach tree poison, draw blood leaf, stinging leaf bush, Jack Spaniard tree, wait in the road come night time bird. I make up these names for Adela' things. I used to keep them in my head for Adela because I get to find out that Adela forget she true true name and she tongue before she leave this earth. I think deep about how a place name Nowhere could make sense and I discover that Adela had to make her mind empty to conceive it. The place she miss must have been full and living and take every corner in she mind so when she reach, there was no more room for here.

Fanning the fire, I used to try to make my mind as empty as Adela' but I never like it because it make me feel lonely and blind and sorrowful and take me away from myself and then I know is so Adela feel when she come here. I used to sit and make all I know, what I seen yesterday and the day before, and even the woman who mind me, pass from my head and when I come back the coals would be out and the day passing across the samaan. When she look at this place it remind her of nowhere for is not a place that is easy to get out of and it don't look like any other place. Mountains cut all sides, river run like ribbons, rock to one side, the sea near enough to smell and far enough to desire. All the way here, Adela, registering the stench of the ship, must have memorize the road to find she way out and the road was not only solid ground but water too, and so long it take, true is not time it take, is wrack and pull. So long she had time to balance the oceans and measure how much mouthful she would have to swallow to get back but when she reach and find sheself locked in on all sides and not by nothing human, she drop, she call it Nowhere and begin to forget by forgetting the road, cut into the mountain valley, the walls of immortelle and bamboo, green and wet, the hundred rivers gutting the road, the mark she put on the red dirt under the cart, the wheel turning, turning near she face where they lay she down, the water raining down in that valley in mist. They lay she down in that cart because every minute she wanted to jump, is what. But every different place they put her she take an opportunity to remember all the things that she was going to forget. For Adela was remembering that and long before that, back to the ship. She calculate their face and she calculate their heart. But all that calculation come to a stop when she reach nowhere. Everything after the narrow passage to the new world, the tunnel to the ship where only one body could pass, everything after the opening, the orange rim of dirt, jutting at her eye, which was the rest and first of what she was, she lose. Her powers come small and she done breathe right here. All her maps fade from her head, washing off from zinnia to pale ink, the paper of ways, that she stitch and stick with saliva and breath, rinse as the sky in June come watery; the blue of Guinea, her mark for horizon, wash out; the red dirt under the cart, all the weight and balance and measure, at which point she had ordered the species in grains of sand, thinned to brown; the brocade heft of clouds, the wonderful degrees of light, all that done vanish. She could not hold on to the turquoise sea what bring she here. Everything pour out of she eyes in a dry, dry river. Everything turn to lime and sharp bones, and she didn't catch sheself until it was she true name slipping away.

Cool cool it leave she, so cool. It leave like breeze, dark with more wanderings, dark with destination and dark with she life. Destination, yes. It leave going it' own way. Cool cool it slip her memory and it vanish. All what remain now is how to calculate breathing. Her heart just shut. It shut for rain, it shut for light, it shut for water and it shut for the rest of we what follow. Adela feel something harder than stone and more evil than sense. Here.

Much later I myself get to understand when I look and see with my own eyes Verlia in flight, feel red explosion in my heart draining me of tenderness. I know it don't have no word for what happen then just as it don't have none now. I know Adela set her mind to stopping her breath after that.

Verlia leave me like nothing too. Like nothing. One minute I see her standing there on the edge of the cliff and the minute I turn my head she was gone. She was always hard to hold on to, always she would leave me in the middle of a conversation or in the middle of a word, in the middle of my hand opening for her. She would move so fast to the junction she would vanish. She would slip into air quick, quick any time I turn to meet her. She never learn to take the world as it is. She never want to make do with what there was.

When she name gone from her, the woman I was given to say that Adela walk out of Nowhere and gone to where nobody know. Naked as she born. Not another word was heard of her though they say she must have gone up to Moriah and past. She part the envious darkness with her foot. She climb the silk cotton tree up there and fly all the way back to Africa. She bend over deep deep in her own worries, so deep. But I could not put my foot in that darkness when the time come though I envy Adela.

I get to find out these things as a child and in my smallness all I could think was how the names of things would make this place beautiful. I dreaming up names all the time for Adela' things. I dream Adela' shape. I even get to talking to she as if she there and asking how she like this one or that one. Tear up cloth flowers, stinking fruit tree, draw blood bush, monkey face flowers, hardback swamp fish. I determine to please she and recall. Slippery throat peas, wet sea fern, idle whistle bird, have no time bird. Is a lot of bird to name — busy wing, better walking, come by chance, wait and see, only by cocoa, only by cane, scissors' tail, fire throat, wait for death. I say to myself that if I say these names for Adela it might bring back she memory of herself and she true name. And perhaps I also would not feel lonely for something I don't remember.

Thinking in this way the rain would sweep me before I pick up the clothes from the stone bleach, the wind would take the line, I would leave the rice burning on the stove thinking, the sky reflect the continents today, Adela, there is Africa and Madagascar, there is Moriah and there Parlatuvier, there Saint Michel and Gros Islet, Choiselle, Fyzabad, Ninth Company. It seem like the clouds is hard enough to be land there Adela, the sky full of Sahara dust that blow quite here they say Adela. Adela, rain ants coming to cover we in water. Nothing barren here, Adela, in my eyes everything full of fullness, everything yielding, the milk of yams, dasheen bursting blue flesh. Sometimes the green overwhelm me too Adela, it rise wet and infinite on both sides of me as a vault of bamboo and immortelle and teak. Adela, the samaan was my mother. She spread and wave and grow thicker. Is you I must thank for that. Where you see nowhere I must see everything. Where you leave all that emptiness I must fill it up. Now I calculating.

Though often and still I know the feeling what Adela

feel when she reach, the purposelessness of recalling come big in my throat, for the place beautiful but at the same time you think how a place like this make so much unhappiness. But since then I make myself determined to love this and never to leave.

What she recalled was the empty spaces below the beds, the
wood floor, the smell of antiseptic, the breeze through the
window, the thin iron legs of the hospital beds, the rows of
them with the spaces underneath where the breeze blew, the
beds looking suspended from the floor by the breeze, the
shine wood, the woman they'd given her away to lying on the
bed, her mouth sagging in a stroke, the white starchy sheets,
the linen the woman she'd been given to saved for her dying,
the embroidered pillow case, the lace handkerchief hanging
on to the woman's now bony fingers, the fingers she didn't
recognize, saffron root thin, lace and root, her feet swinging
above the floor, in the breeze, the coolness in it, the sand in
it, the smell of rain somewhere far off, the heat through the
window, the pooled sun under the beds, the woman she'd
been given to murmuring nothing, her fingers rooted in the
lace like another place, a place she was already going to, part
of her already there, dust in the sun's shafts, cracked, friz-
zled, fly light through her eyelashes, the thought that this
would be over soon, when she woke up, if this was sleep but

it wasn't, and the woman who took her was lying in stiff white linen which she had ironed and sprinkled over with blessed water. She went to the window, the smell of sickness in her nostrils, on her fingers, on the lace in her hand, the one good lace handkerchief of the woman they'd given her to sticking to her fingers when she raised her thumb to her mouth at the window. What she recalled was the window then the bed and her body curled underneath after the window and her thumb, sucking lace, the bolt of the bed and the sheet tight as a skirt and the floor shine and scratched from her shoe. She, under the bed, the woman above, the thread of the kerchief close to her eyes like thick rope, her shoe black and patent-leathered below her knee, the woman sagging in the bed. The thought that she was sitting here with the lace until the woman minding her called her. Come here, pull out that finger, eat before they say I make you starve, you hear girl. The doorway which she would not leave, the lace left her or the window that was not home, the woman above clutching the blued earth of where she is going, the close smell of rain, the thought to run pick up the clothes.

The thought slipping away and darting back that the lady was leaving her by herself, she would not be back and the woman was all that she knew, her shiny patent-leather shoes dangling from the bed, her feet bunching out like yams, the white socks bursting, her knees dry and spindly, the woman who'd taken her, eyelids pulling themselves open, not recognition but still impatience as go get water, shut off the tap now light the fire wash yourself girl don't drag the clothes pump the lamp get the kerosene come straight home walk quick before it get dark close the door draw the curtain, impatience meant she was still here, with her, but sometimes the woman's eyes rolled away, her fingers clutching lace, scratching the dirt of the place she was going, it was already under her nails, in the saliva silvering on her lips and well rid of this world, murmuring. What she recalled was her lack of surprise that the woman who took her wanted to go.

The woman they'd given her to — well not really given because she was not a gift just a mouth to feed — left her, left her at the door, with her legs ash dry with not eating. The woman they left her with was the woman with a market garden. They left her at the door everyday and one day no one returned to get her. She remembers and remembers until she remembers nothing but the woman's face, the round black eyes, the mouth chewing chewing, the milk of coconut at the corners and her hands thick and soft but stinging when she hit. The woman talked and chewed saying, "What they think it is at all, I just have enough for me. I make any child, I ask for child, if I wanted child I woulda make child. This child can't even work self. They just bring she here to eat me out. I make any child. Child go get the water. I minding big snake. I want any child. Look here tie up your bundle and put it under the bed, this house is not a thoroughfare. I look like I want any child?"

She does not remember them, only voices hastening her towards the house and saying stay there. She remembers two of them coming to play with her under the tree and hitting her and running away from her, out of her reach on the rope round the samaan tree. She remembers looking forward to seeing them every morning when the woman who kept her went away until they started hitting, poking her with a switch. She remembers pleasure at their coming until they came. It would wash over her warm when she heard their voices through the bush jingling like nails on stone and they would kiss her and chase her around the tree until she could not breathe and then they would hit her and run. She thinks they were her brother and sister. They must have been. She would forget that they hit her the minute she heard their voices coming in the mid-morning. She anticipated their hands on her cheeks, their murmuring how fat and pretty she was, their pinches, their games.

"You close your eyes, you spin around ten times then open them and look up at the sky. No. No, come this way then walk three steps then spin."

"Here, three ants, we'll put them on we tongue, see who get bite first. Who don't get bite is a jumbie."

"If the gooje fall on the line you out and no stepping on the line neither. See the line here, your foot right here, that's out."

"If you ever do something wrong, spin round three times then throw three stones over your back. You wouldn't get licks. True, true."

"Tell the lady to take we too," they'd say to her. "Promise, promise, tell she to take we. Then we go play with you all the time, day and night. Don't forget to tell she, you hear!"

Up the hill, up in the bush she would send her ears to hear where they came from; she would send her ears behind them when they left so she could hear the first crumble of hog grass in the morning saying that they were coming back. She listened at night, listened for them eating or washing their feet or playing without her, she listened and listened. When they stopped coming she did not hear. And then she forgot them but remembered listening and jingling and breathlessness from running after them.

"These people make all sorts of children for other people to take care of. I come in the world alone. Anybody ever give me anything? Anybody ever leave me anything? They ever even spit in their hand and say, 'look dog'? Not a penny, not a piece of bread not even a memory."

They said that the woman's hands had luck, anything grew under them, they said she had money in her mattress, they said her brassière overflowed with money not breasts. "I have nothing. What I have is for me one, not other people' burden. I never make a child yet God help me. If I wanted child I would a make child, you don't see." But she'd taken her in if only to wipe her bitterness up, if only to sop it like bread in milk, her mouth working the cussing like chewing. If only to feel something human in the room listening.

"You have a name girl?"

"Elizete, Miss."

"Who is you now? Where you come out?"

"Me en't know."

"You en't know, eh? You en't know."

Taken her, washing her face in it every day. Who else came close enough to touch, who else came close enough to hear her venom. "God make all Adela' children woman and all her generations and now they come and drop a girl child on me. You see how that woman curse we."

Who could come. Only sent. To this woman who looked like plenty but when she opened her mouth it was stingy. "Ragtail girl child, as if we don't suffer enough. I don't have nothing for you. I only have for me. I say I was the end of that woman, but they come and drop this child staring at me with she face. Look at my cross. Turn your face, turn your face to the wall when I come in this room."

Who else. Only sent. As what couldn't be sent in blood no longer. This woman had seen to that. Tied up her womb in brackish water. Drink cassava tea from the first day. Starch it stiff. Anything now would have to come from spirit. Who else.

She waited quietly, she did not move otherwise the woman would not speak. She practised waiting without moving, the hair on the back of her neck poised, her breathing almost still.

"They drop this child on me and never once look back. They bring you even a sweetie?"

She always stood facing the wall in the evening when the woman wanted to talk but did not want to acknowledge her presence as if acknowledging would be like loving and she didn't want loving. And she didn't want Elizete to imagine loving so she gave her the wall to face, the wood knots and wood lice trails. "Adela." Elizete would listen for her name tracing the grainy wood lice tunnels on the wall. She would stand as she was told, her back to the room waiting to hear Adela's name, waiting to hear the woman say how Adela leave, how Adela long gone, how Adela leave blight, how Adela... She tried to work out the geometry of the sandy paths up the wall where the wood was softened by the chewing of wood lice. She tried to trace them home, yet perhaps home was these paths, she thought, or their way of not being seen, waiting and listening. The woman's voice behind her always ending in questions. She tried not to move so that the woman would not be distracted and would head straight for Adela. If she kept still enough, she would hear about Adela. If she concentrated hard enough on tracing the tunnels and not moving her arms or her head and not breathing loudly, all of which disturbed the woman, the woman would talk about Adela. Turned to the wall she could feel the story crawl over her shoulders and up her neck, she could feel it like something brown and sweet making the hair at her neck tremble. Something thick like cake. She cut out the bitterness in the woman's voice, she put it down that it was because the woman had been left, by everyone. How else was there no one here but them? And being left, waiting for nails on stone was left. She cut out the way the woman wrung out the words, as if wringing a dress dry, her voice would stretch and squeeze. She was glad she faced the wall. She did not want to see her mouth dry as a dress waist. She caught her words, as soon as they were thrown, taking the dress waist and soaking it in water again, drenching it in the dampness of Moriah, the air standing in water in Moriah, filling it out to the full bloom of Adela, each time the story came towards her standing against the wall. She never tired; she caught it over and over again, filled it billowy and wet.

"She gone, yes, she leave we here to suffer."

She knew that the woman talked loudly not to reach her at the wall but because she was really talking to the spirits, her tone saying to them, "Keep your business to yourself," knowing that the rooms, the fields were always full of everyone. And the room never paid attention to the woman's tone. It confused her or angered her more that no one answered, that the walls remained sullen, stubborn to her talk and that turning she would find only Elizete conspiring with the wood lice. She would tie her head up and soak it with bay rum and almost reach a scream, turning on everything, the chair, the stove, the broomstick. And Elizete would brace her back for licks and the woman calling out something she had done wrong last week or yesterday, not knowing that she could not lift her hand against Elizete without tiring or feeling more pain in her head because Elizete had already prepared. Threw three stones over her shoulder at the door, one spin under the samaan tree before. Elizete's small magic. Throwing words was asking for answers, the woman knew, banding her head, her temper rising. It was summoning the spirits, getting on their nerves. Until they pushed through her own lips and let her words bite her. Until her head ached with the ring of stone, the jingle of old iron. Whenever her hand wasn't in solid soil mashing it up and kneading it down her temper rose and her head ached. She pushed her hands in for the cool feel of earth, for the black feel of it to surge in her arms and to quiet her. She did her planting not standing up but sitting down, solid and spread out, the dasheen root, the yam root between her legs and both arms plunged in the soil. This is how her yield was plenty, soaked in sweat, her dress heavy with provisions. All that temper, all that disagreeableness, kneading and tamping and burrowing, it was the smell like burnt bread and green crushed leaves that quieted her. The deeper she pushed, the richer, the more secret; mingling with the sweat of her arms, the fresh rush of must, the suck of black earth where she was going. Come evenings when she had to rise up, pull her hands from the soil, slow her sweat, the woman they'd left her with would be miserable and throwing words for Elizete and the spirits.

"It was Adela and then...then it was some...plenty, with no name. And then it had Evelyn and Marie and Drummond and Cipriani and Martial and José Emanuel, and Wilfred and Samson and Doraline and Victory and Valiant and Rosamund and Felicity and Baby and me after Baby, Mirelda Josefena. All dead or might as well. And born unhappy and blight. Mal jo." And she was the last she know about or wanted to. Up here so much changing from dry red dirt to wet. Nothing stay except hardness. Now they send give she some little girl, not even blood but spitting image as she recall and she recall by heart. Adela.

"Bring girl child here to swell up on me. I hope they know. Jumbie girl. Don't let me have to see your face, you hear me. Let them just stay out of my house."

She wished that the woman were kinder. Talked softer, coaxed the spirits instead of giving them offence.

"Not in my place. Let them come out."

She wanted her to talk about Adela, talk like Adela would talk. She imagined Adela talk, she dreamed her talking without a word, soft soft.

"Better she than me. Yes. Leave is all I…she could think of.
All the marks on she…me is for thinking of leaving. Each
time she…I see leaving I…you could not stop it. As if my
hand was out of control or heading for where it ought to be,
as easy as if it was coming to rest at my…she side. Leave…
I…she ought to be a woman her dress tail disappearing
toward the dense rain forest of Tamana going to my life, she
marronnage, rain, drenched, erasing footfalls 'is so things is' I
say, for the night dew heavy like a damp fig-leafed wall but
more merciful. If this was enough to crack a world it was
sufficient to close one, to make a passage of me that only get
glimpse like an evening closing, yet. Her mouth taste the
cool charm of a stone past and I determine to stop this
imperfect persistence of flesh jostling the air. Now this time
I…she dreamless, she…I done imagining. Leave is all I
could think to do. My hand don't follow me, every piece of
she have a mind by itself. I…she say is so things is. I dreamless. I see my hair taken to the four corners of the earth. The
parts of me fly 'way, my head could not hold them together.
I don't belong here but even where I…she belong I cannot
remember after a while. As this thing happen my eyes close
on me, my back turn on she…me, my heart close. Is so
things is. Leave is all she could think so much she wasn't
there. What it matter to think in this flesh. It feel like my
yoke. Nothing come to me of what is happening, nothing
tell me that everyday open for light or my belly open for

children. These things is too ordinary and long past what she...my life is now and they is even a bother and only a moment to pass. I see how I...she could not think of them that come out of me for I...she was not there no more and let the dead bury the dead. She who name I...she forget."

Adela' voice hovered on their hot cold lips, the two of them, one standing at the wall tracing wood lice the other her head in bay rum, her mouth working coconut to milk. Light would out and she is still standing at the wall where the woman told her to and the woman with the head of pain is still cussing anything in her way, even the draft through the floor boards, the first cry of cicadas. As how she had been left a head that pained her and that would only stop for her hands in the earth, and how throwing words was no use to a woman long dead and gone and who never was here; and how the trouble with the dead is they don't care and this world don't mean nothing to them; and how she'd been left a tongue that any devil want to light on and take liberty. She falls asleep standing up before the woman releases her, drooped and half awake she murmurs more names for Adela — donkey eye stone, blue finger yam....

"Don't waste your time. Nobody have no mother nobody have no father and everybody big and have their sense and I was the end of her line so they better not bring no more child for me."

She is a stray child left here because the woman has breasts that look like money and her hands grow fat yams and dasheen. A stray, wandering as strays wander, their eyes or fancy hitting on a piece of wood, a door, the smell of fish or meat, wandering until they linger and forget where they were going, or until they remember another smell or patch of yard, another house; until in the middle of remembering they forget and alight where they are; a stray wandering until something struck her about the house or the samaan tree in front. Perhaps tilting her head to catch a certain light through her lashes, then noticing her cheek angle to the plain of the door. Again, perhaps the woman once knew her mother, perhaps the pumpkin vine running down the hill sprung her, perhaps they were passing friends, her mother and the woman, or perhaps there was never any formality or acquaintance. Perhaps her mother forgot her there, walking up the hill, just forgot her, letting her hand go to point the way, move a branch, look at a nettle pricking her foot, just forgot her. Her mother, one midday, resting at the woman's yard, flicking sweat from her face and then turning up the hill again forgetting the bundle she had laid down. And it might have been more deliberate. Her mother walking by seeing the woman's garden — not flowers, provisions — made a sign, remarked on the garden. "You have a nice garden there, neighbour." Once, perhaps they stared at each other. The one having to get something from the house giving out for one moment that she was looking, the other needing to leave something. Then one day leaving her there with a cloth bundle of her few belongings or nothing but the clothes on her back, knowing that this was how people lived here, passing children and food and necessity and word onto each other. Here, there was no belonging that was singular, no need to store up lineage or count it; all this blood was washed thick and thin, rinsed and rinsed and rubbed and licked and stained; all this blood gashed and running like rain, lavered and drenched and sprinkled and beat upon clay beds and cane grass. No belonging squared off by a fence, a post, or a gate. Not in blood, not here, here blood was long and not anything that ran only in the vein. Every stranger was looked over for signs and favour. If you came upon this place suddenly, curious gazes would search your face for family. Hmm, mouths would turn down in recognition; there was always something for someone, long dead or long gone, long lost, long time, in the faces: "That one went away when?" "She reach back now, oui." "She self." Away, not necessarily this earth but away; eyes that favoured a dead soul, ears; messages from the dead in the way a thumb was sucked, the way a head inclined, braid hanging; there was the way a baby leaned or turned her head, the way a newborn's eyes looked as if she'd been here already.

"That one Virgie?"

"That one Dan?"

"That one Estelle."

"No, God, that one is Adela self. But where she come from now? En't she leave this place?"

"Look nah this child is the spitting image, spitting spitting image of Adela."

She appeared in straight-backed, stiff-kneed children who wanted to walk before they could crawl, in babies who refused food and died within a week of their arrival, their lips pursed and rigored, in children who wouldn't keep their clothes on, wanted to take them off to go walking in the big road, in two-year-olds in love with an axle, bolting in front a lorry, and in forgetfulness, the way gazing out a window a girl would let the rice burn, the way walking to the standpipe a woman would catch up in a conversation and then stare at the empty bucket curiously, the way wanting her back scratched a woman would call out every name that she'd given her children except the one she'd meant to call. No, no, belonging was not singular. They were after belonging. Long past. They had had enough of it anyway, their bellies were runny with it. Enough of love too. So much of it that they sucked their teeth at it. Useless. That's what it was. Unnecessary. Passing. Worse, you couldn't eat it. Never helped anything. It never brought anyone back from the dead or from the living. And this was the heart of it and the same. What would it matter if the girl burning the rice at the window knew her great-great-grandmother? Nothing. She would have to know before that not to burn the rice, not to stare out the window so vacantly, not to be drawn to the window at all. That woman near the standpipe would not decide finally that the bucket was a gorge and ready, catch her foot against the pebble of it and dive. No, no. She would have to know long before. Love was too simple — just knowledge, immediately felt about the immediate place, but the girl burning the rice at the window needed history, something before this place, something that this place cut off. At the heart. And the woman with the bucket, well at the heart there was no bucket, and no woman either. They had not come here willingly looking for food or water or liking the way the place set off against the sky or even for hunger. They had not come because the hunting was good or the ground moist for planting. They had not come moving into the forest just after the rainy season. They had not come because they saw great cities foreshadowed in the horizon or rum shops sprawling with their dancing and laughter. Not because a shape overtook them in geometry or because after observing speeding clouds they coveted a new landfall. They had been taken. Plain. Hard. Rough. Swept up from thinking of the corn to be shucked, the rains coming or no rain coming at all for the season, that patch of high grass to clear. The mist gathering at their feet. The steam of baking. Poised over a well, the bag lowered, they had been plucked, or, caught in the misfortune of a wedding or a war, sold.

Well, true. They had had so much of love that they were numb to the sweet smells of the Atlantic at Moriah and its offensive colour. No blizzard of aquamarine could sooth them, not even teeming with fish. They had had enough of aimless boats and bodies tangled bone-white exhaling colour to black coral. And enough of distance too, distance without cover, Jesus, without a sky, without a hiding place, finite distance, God, islands, islands that came to an end, distance that ran out. Feet hanging, slipping over the edge, ran out. Plain. There were no interiors, no outposts, no relief. No hiding for the flatness, no hiding for the end. There was a valley and hillsides and crops, and crops of children, crops enough to bury and plant and grow again because really there is no ending, ending is only something we hope for like darkness, and bush trails and blood trails...blood trees. Places they skirted for many years. "Never walk here, you will raise the dead and they will follow you home or make you lose your way." Places where someone was hung, places that didn't need description or writing down. Certainly not owning. And belonging? They were past it. It was not wide enough, not gap enough, not distance enough. Not rip enough, belonging. Belonging was too small, too small for their magnificent rage. They had surpassed the pettiness of their oppressors who measured origins speaking of a great patriarch and property marked out by violence, a rope, some iron; who measured time in the future only and who

collectivity

discarded memory like useless news. They owned the sub-
lime territory of rage. Such rage it would hawk and spit out
a grass-throated ocean, islands choking; so much it would
long for a continent to wash up on and to chastise. They
were not interested in belonging. It could not suffice. Not
now. It could not stanch the gushing ocean, it could not
bandage the streaming land. They saw with the bloodful
clarity of rage.

So they saw everything. Heard everything, abandoned
distance, abandoned time and saw everything. They saw
nothing could be done. That is how they lived with the dead.
That is how they observed their goings on, their comings,
their lingering, their returns. Look at how that broom fell
across the door, see the stones' orderly plan across the road
this morning, out of nowhere, feel the warmth in that part
of the road between Choiselle and Ninth Company, between
the walls before the big tree, when you smell a lily-of-the-
night out of nowhere, tell me that is not someone lingering;
did somebody call my name? Walking along a deserted track,
footfalls, chain dragging late late, this door, this door don't
want to be opened, who there, who there, the window gust-
ing wide and the oil bottle just fall down and break so. That
is how they dealt in the thoughts of everyone who had
existed for five hundred years, everyone who was brought
here left here since Adela's time and left their thoughts in the
air, unable to leave since leaving would suggest a destination

and where they had to go was too far and without trace and without maps and there was something that needed to be settled and haunted too. And then they were trapped, the way even spirits could be trapped like the living. And the living, they lived in the past or had no past but a present that was filled, peopled with the past. No matter their whims and flights into the future some old face or old look, some old pain would appear.

So the child standing under the samaan had to be taken in. If she didn't move as the dark was gathering, if she could not remember where she had come from but stood under the samaan waiting, then the woman at the door watching had to beckon her. Not before waiting though, seeing if the dark would run her home, not before saying "You still there girl? Why you don't go? I want any jumbie in my house?" And the girl, standing there under the samaan, afraid to move out of the range of a human voice, out of the range of the small light from the kitchen door, said nothing. Just stood as if she'd been spun around and the world was upside-down. Just stood as if she'd lost her direction. The woman beckoned her from the door, not before saying "Go away girl. Go away spirit. I didn't send call you. Shoo!" Not before peeping out to see if she was still there, after singing a song to show she was not afraid, her life was going on inside the door and no spirit was going to unnerve her, just come and drop themself here as if what? "Ay Ay! I have any time for this? I have to get up in the morning you know girl! Go home jumbie girl!" The girl stood still, scared of moving, scared of standing still, her face scarred salt. The woman peering at her from the kitchen. The woman beckoned.

She'd landed up here though, the square mall of the donut shop, gape open to the road and iron Canadian National that she didn't even know yet was a railroad, or had been; she'd only seen it blooded with rust, smelted out of the side of the donut shop, frozen in mottled iron wall, dropped into the street below. And across from the mall, a hotel, the Gladstone, bar underneath, no windows, just the blast of country music each time the door opened, carpets, stinking of shoes, piss, beer, the soar, foam and lashing waves of alcohol thrown up. Where one morning outside a white woman hung on to the bus-stop pole, backing off a stumbling white man, her purse held up high. In the mornings the Gladstone looked like somebody caught opening a door that should have been left shut, like things well left alone, like Saturday night clothes, all rumpled and slept in with somebody still wearing them Sunday morning. Landed up and saw as anyone would see now. Anyone like her. She saw nothing or she saw the raw surface. Everything was raw, her skin, her mouth, her eyes, her heart. Everything she saw was raw, caked over with grime, the raw promise of trade the whole night, giving up the part of your body that was worth nothing and something all at once and hoping no one would take you up on it, not for a lousy drink, not with the beer spilling on the tables, the stink of the place, not with your eyes avoiding the floor and the corners and the man next to you who says he has a room, his pores waxed over, fused into paste with booze. But all that was perhaps later for Elizete. Another life. Not today. Today she was Columbus, today the Canadian National was not the Canadian National yet and the Gladstone was not a bar and nothing had a name yet, nothing was discovered. She'd never end up swinging on the bus-stop pole backing away a man though something about the dingy drop into blooded iron and the rising shoulder of the Gladstone and the factories after that hank of rail told her that this little square of mall could not float her too long. But she'd landed here.

Land up yes. Look at my cross. It can't make no sense except like a fish floating and ending up wherever the eternal sea take it. Just as you think you have a hold of life it bounce you over a canefield, a cliff, a whole damn ocean. Just as you have a hold it knock you down. Just so. Just as you get something they take it.

Landed like a fish or a ship. More like fish on somebody's line than ship. Less like fish because she couldn't swim hard enough to cover that mall, all one acre of it, swim like if she wasn't going to stay here. She'd have to look new every morning, like she lived somewhere, to keep away the police and her own doubt which was even more dangerous. She'd have to pretend that she was an eccentric, not a woman way past down on her luck and raw in the stomach, but a woman with a notebook and pencil, maybe keeping a diary. But she couldn't even come up with the coffee, and her notebook was a collection of brown paper bags she kept just in case. Collected in case…you never know. People here waste things and one day when she got her self back she would need them. Somebody would come home and need one and she'd have it. So she swam, reeled in, sprouting legs to crawl all over that mall, looking like a regular, making the cops take notice, a crack head they figured, not homeless, countryless, landless, nameless. No. Crack head. The light of their cruiser deadeying her each night sliding into the donut shop.

Her feet scraped over the mall, by the pizza shop watching the customers in the daytime, waiting for them to leave the ridge of dough at the fat end of the slice on the table. Her hand would sweep over as she walked casually by, wasting her broadest smile on the boy gone back to flattening out another crust, not paying her any mind really. This city didn't pay any mind, everybody looked straight ahead of themselves. Eyes never hit a corner or anything hard to watch, never took in the whole world which is why since landing at that mall it had been three weeks and she'd faded, she hoped, into the concrete and glass. She'd worked each angle of it, the pizzeria till five, the Van Dong restaurant till eleven and the video arcade in the afternoons. She was working edges. If she could straighten out the seam she'd curled herself into, iron it out like a wrinkle, sprinkle some water on it and then iron it out, careful, careful not to burn....

Months and she still hadn't heard about Yonge Street because she hadn't looked that way, just stared at the hank of Canadian National and the factories beyond. Nobody told her about Yonge Street or Avenue Road or Yorkville. Nobody told her what wasn't necessary or possible or important for a woman from nowhere. She'd been told about kitchens and toilets and floors and sewing machines and cuffs and rubber and paint spray and even been offered some sidewalks but nobody told her about any place she wouldn't fit in. And this mall that she was crawling over was only here because she didn't have a new card, a name to find her way into one of the places she was made for.

She did not know the city, would never know it because she wasn't looking at it. Who could see? If it was there she would see. She knows about seeing. But it was just something across her brow, something she made a movement to brush away like a piece of hair or a cobweb. She would never miss it because she would never know it. Missing was something she'd had enough of already. Missing and wanting had been emptied out of her. All of here was just something brushing across her brow. The only thing that she kept was hanging on and that was involuntary. She had no control of it. So when she found herself creeping around a mall and hanging on she could not stop. She wished that the police would take her in, send her somewhere but she hid from them, involuntary too. She could not help but make a way, just ... well, she hung on.

Months in some place just for the whiff of another human being she'd had a glimpse of. Well, who'd given her a glimpse just enough to haunt her. Haunt her into dropping here like a stone. Stone. She tried to mash her own face in with a stone when Verlia went. She'd held it in her hand and pounded and pounded, but Verlia was still gone. Over and over the stone in her hand moved to the pulp of her mouth, hoping.

Months and one day she just had to get off this main street where she seemed to be in public view. One day, after the Gladstone had called her and she'd sat inside at a table drinking a rum. She had asked for it and felt at home. "A rum." Saying the word made the room familiar. The waitress did not understand her at first so she said it again. "A rum." Making all that brown bitter warmth repeat in her throat, her face heat up. When it came plain and brown it didn't seem the same. Not the same as at the little shop in Moriah, the half window open except on Thursdays where the shopkeeper would slosh it over his fingers and into your glass and throw a corkful back himself leaving the bottle on the sill. She stared at it when it came, how little it was, how without the generous slosh, the one for the spirits. Even the brown didn't seem the same. There the heat melted it amber. After a moment she threw it back and wiped her hand across her mouth, feeling the coarse stream of it pass into her chest. The familiar burning sat her still, hummed in her face like back home. Though it wasn't back home, it was a room thick and brown in a city somewhere and there was no sound like calling, no sound like a voice lifted or thinning through any window. No sound of a body turning in bed to look at a window where she was standing. "Just so, just so as if I wasn't there waiting." No sound not even of the city outside, the cars, the dense noise. Just she sitting in a chair anywhere. But it wasn't anywhere it was somewhere. She was sitting somewhere drinking a rum imagining another place, a woman she'd had a fight with that morning whose absence flattened the arc of her cutlass, a rumkeeper's hand washed in amber, his red eyes, the brief counter of the rum shop, just a shack with a ledge, a door half open, her hand knocking the shot back, wiping her mouth on her shoulder, heading home. Heading home found her sitting here, the swig of rum on her chest, hard hard, too hard to head home. She could not remember where it was or ever going there without uncertainty. Someone slid into the chair beside her, furry and heavy and another rum went down her amber chest. Some-one said something, she didn't hear, her face felt heavy, no, numb, tired, then she wanted to get up and something lay on her arm. Wood, skin, was it her arm, there was someone she wanted to think about, she was lost watching hair, skin, the wood of the chair, khaki. Her face was on the table, glass, yes rain outside, get the clothes quick....

She'd landed here in this maze of streets behind the mall, passing by, passing all the houses where something was going on, a life, a regular beat, a certain gospel she had not learned. Not here, not there. She saw it. People making life with each other; adding a girl here, a boy there, a cousin, a neighbour; eating breakfast, playing checkers, slapping dominoes as if they knew or rather shared something, some gift. She walked down the back streets, as if she was going somewhere and each succeeding day it would take her longer to find her way back to the mall. Nowhere to go. Made her feel that there was something malformed about her. Like something someone had forgotten, misplaced because it did not catch their eye. It put her back to the nervous sweat of childhood, the burning under her feet, standing, waiting to be taken in. Wonder of the world, stinging nettle, donkey eye, thirsty throat, bois cano, blood tree, sick river, red ants, batchac, drought cracked, looking for water. No amount of stories and made up things would hide this sense for long. It did not matter, when she really pondered it.

Something in the way but not bothersome or important, the way being graceless makes what you do not seen, and maybe someone would come along and move her, place her where they felt she ought to be. Not for favour but just to rearrange the yard, the kitchen; send her to fetch a needle, some thread, a stalk of cane, a cup of water. Before she could remember, a feeling waiting for her all the time, a feeling that she had been staving off when Verl left her and when there was just the cliff gaping open. But before that. When she arrived, before she knew herself and it came tied to a tree, standing against a wall, filling the water bucket at the standpipe, beckoned across a yard when darkness was gathering and her face crusting into salt, now walking this street in another country. She didn't know where it had come from, had someone said it, had someone put it on her like a blight, a light, or like rubbing her back with aloes to soothe her. She doesn't remember making it up herself just taking it like she took her hand, her legs, her fingers, across the yard from the samaan tree; she doesn't remember being sorry for it just understanding it as understanding the rain, the morning.

Each day it would take her longer to find her way back to the mall. Each day she travelled another street further and further into the maze; she thought that she could smell the sea as she moved along the grid of pavements and alleys and houses all the same, brown bricked windows sealed forever.

She thought that she was heading for the sea. But then she came to buildings with no people and a wide road like the one with the Gladstone waiting. She tasted rum in her throat and moved back into the maze of streets again.

Once a woman speaking another language let her sleep in the back of a house. She left in the early morning when she woke up to a girl looking at her through a window. If she stood in between the houses after it was dark and everyone had gone to sleep, and very quietly, she could make a bed of what she carried then wake up before they awoke and leave.

Heavy as hell. Her body. She doesn't want a sense of it while she's living on the street.

She doesn't think of the scars on her legs, she doesn't hide them, she doesn't think of Verlia touching them, pressing the soft hollows of her feet, she doesn't hide them as she had from Verlia. She doesn't want to remember the morning waking up and finding Verlia touching them. She doesn't want to remember the look in Verlia's eyes, of pity. How she hated that look and understood it, how she pulled her legs away, how she said "No!", how Verlia looked as if she did not know what she had done. Of course there was a distance between them that was inescapable and what they did not talk about. At times she saw someone she did not know in Verlia. Someone too cool, not from here, someone who felt pity for people less capable. How could she know Verlia. All she'd seen was a bit of black and bright yellow pass her eyes and sweat raining glad. The only time that sweat looked pure and willing. And wanting to touch it, wipe it off laughing was all.

"Don't feel sorry for me," she'd said, "and don't look at my legs."

All over from one thing and another, one time or another, is how Isaiah whip them for running, is how he wanted to break me from bad habit. Whip. "Don't move." Whip. "Don't move." Whip. "Run you want to run! Don't move." Is how the cane cut them from working. Same rhythm.

She doesn't want to think of Verlia looking at them. Kissing every one as if she wanted them kissed. She didn't want them kissed. It was too easy, too light. She knows that there is no kiss deep enough for that.

"I ask you? Stop it now. Leave me alone."

Then she had tied her feet in their rags and went out to the field, not returning till late and not speaking to Verlia, not even when she lay beside her.

She doesn't want her own body with her now. But she wants Verlia, even her pitying, even her coolness like a draft of cold air passing a doorstep.

In the houses in the maze at night she sees them having supper, she sees women passing across lighted windows, as she had crossed kerosene-lit windows, wiping their hands, as hers, half dressed as she had been half dressed, pausing to remember. And she sees them in the mornings, smells their perfume encasing them in distance again, their faces suddenly glassy, without the ease she'd seen behind the lighted windows. At first she'd thought these women always foreign, always distant. They had a way of looking and not looking, of never being known. They had a way of appearing always dressed, fully clothed, and they never looked at her, or looked at her as one would a child, inquiring what she had done. But she'd seen them cross their windows, rubbing their eyes, in disarray, so they were in the end only full of secrets like her.

That day at the Gladstone she'd ended up in a room with a man. He lay on a bed with blood on his hands. He was asleep. He had one shoe on, the other was on the floor. The room was dark. His eyes were open but he was asleep. They were red, his eyes. He rolled to one side and made a sound; she grabbed his shoe ready to hit him but he was quiet again. She found the door and left. She decided to get away from the mall and the Gladstone and began to walk the maze of streets trying to get to the sea.

Only an inch at a time. And it really wasn't so big but she was learning caution, watching for bad luck, bad eye, goat mouth. So the first place was a room with four others like her, sleeping in shifts, or working in shifts, or sleeping under the bed or in the bathtub or in the chair in the kitchen of the rooming-house or if you had two jobs closing your eyes for a couple hours, head on the table or if, after the two jobs, you were so tired you couldn't sleep and you only saw mops flashing swash swash on your stiffened eyeballs or if you couldn't get rid of the smell of chlorine on your fingers, you stared at the television and learned a new language. Whadya say. They learned this. Watched every show. Game show, talk show, soap opera, Sweet Daddy wrestling The Sheik. All. Everything. After, feeling confident they'd gained something they needed, a key to the day, they'd walk these streets with a natural air, as if they were staying or maybe leaving, with conviction, the key to something definite. How they ticked, how not to be self-conscious, how to...disappear was her intention. Now. Watched everything, melted into the television until they could step out on the street confidently, smiling, secretly, saying to the people they passed, I know you people good now, I can read you Bible, verse and chapter. The TV open up all your business. All how you eat and drink and sleep, all how you treat your family, everything you say, everything you do, all how you born and all how you dead, all how you evil.

The second place — when the first place and the places in between fell apart under suspicion, because suspicion was like air and the only thing you could go on — the second place was a room she shared with a woman, Jocelyn, because it was just two of them and she figured safer. And suspicion was like a person all by itself, weighed as much, had cunning as much. Suspicion could make people disappear from a room without a word or a trace. It could empty a building, crush it or melt it like a secret bomb. It seeped into a perfectly sane and friendly house where at first everybody thought that they were friends and in it together, giving tips on jobs and cheap clothes and then hardly with a word spoken one day because things were going too well, suspicion would seduce the doorway. Someone would lose a job for no good reason they could think of and would suspect someone who didn't pass the butter right, someone they caught looking at them too long, someone they caught using their rice, then it was only a matter of time, everybody knew, from somebody's forgetfulness about where they left their money, to deportation. Or the raid at Athletic Footwear in July that year. Who couldn't believe it wasn't some girlfriend of a man with a girlfriend working there and all their business bust up at Athletic. So much people get caught. All that trampling, the shoes left behind, the coats in the cloak room, the breathlessness in their ears from beating it through the side doors. Couldn't have been the owner who didn't even leave his office, counting the July pay cheques he wouldn't have to pay and closing down for the summer to boot. Who'd complain? Come fall a new crop was waiting no matter what the rumours. And all the converts that the palmists and seers and santerias and obeah people made out of suspicion. The packages buried in single-bible plants under the beds and the tea baths from Chinatown for insurance, because suspicion was not something to play with. The immigration consultants were another story again. Money. And the immigration officers, well they dealt in flesh strictly. So suspicion had a lodging place for good in all the houses on Palmerston and in the mazes of roads ending in wood. Elizete didn't know why the rest of them took it and maybe it was for the same reasons that she did and she rarely asked because that would cause trouble and besides she'd have to be willing to tell her side too. She figured, like her, if they could do better they would. Obeah all around if anyone thought they'd escaped obeah. And if anyone thought the glinty glamour of away, away sent back home in barrels and reeking of some place unscuffed, unmuddy, unrainy; if any of them thought that this was why they came, diving into the gluttony of Honest Ed's would set them straight after a while. But maybe not, because for some it was better than the places they had been, more money. Stepping onto the sidewalk under the garish signs feeling sated and greedy was perhaps better, even if it didn't feed the soul and they spent years outside of themselves, watching other people live, feeling as if they had settled for something less than they were, but what they deserved. They thought that the time would come when they would live, they would get a chance to be what they saw, that was part of the hope that kept them. But ghostly, ghostly this hope, sucking their jaws into lemon seed, kiwi heart, skeletons of pawpaw, green banana stalk. You could see them walking along King, Palmerston, Oakwood, faint. Spines winnowing, ghost seeds, brittling skin flying off, sag on the road...ah, it'll wait...tomorrow...when I was...flour sack sagging, stick bone crackling.... They're not here! All the newspapers bellowing about here, all the traffic lights trying to keep them awake, all the clerks and officers and trainees handling them like paper, folding them in file cabinets. They're not here! By the time they walked these streets they were scraps and bits, shavings.

All the way up they'd gotten used to the idea. Over the turquoise, sipping Grenadines, Marie Galante, Martinique, Guadeloupe's cinched waist and the Caribbean sea where it drowned in the Atlantic. They were Third World people going to the white man country. That in itself lowered them in their own estimation, they could not hope to look forward to being treated right. Already what affected them was getting an inhuman quality. Already nobody was interested in whether they felt mixed up or fucked up. Already their stories were becoming lies because nobody wanted to listen, nobody had the time. That's what happens to a story if nobody listens and nobody has the time, it flies off and your mouth stays open. You end up being a liar because what you say doesn't matter. And there's no tracing or lasting to your stories. They had to end somewhere and another life had to be started and the stories had to be tucked away or secreted away or pressed down because they wandered off in reasons. Their thoughts belonged to wood and this place belonged to metal. They felt each morning as someone trundling a wheelbarrow and pulling a donkey as sleek cars whipped by. They felt each morning as two people — one that had to be left behind and the other. The other was someone they had to get to know, the other was someone they were sometimes ashamed of.

That day she saw a man in the movie house get up and sit down and get up and sit down again. She decided then, the movie was a slip. As she came out of the movie house she could swear the bobbing man followed her home, she could swear she saw him there as she left later that night for work, she could swear that she saw him the day after and the day after and the day after that and the week after and the day they got raided. Then she slid like a fish, out the back door, while they handcuffed the men. Like a fish, no clothes, no shoes, no nothing, air for water, asphalt for feet, floated right back into the mall with the hank of railway and the Gladstone waiting. Caught, caught in just suggestion, suspicion and question, why, why has she come here and it's the same for everyone, all the ones she shares rooms with and all of the ones she shares the style of half their lives cut off.

She has too much to tell. That's the answer, too much she

holds and no place to put it down that would be safe. And why she hasn't met this woman who might rescue her, because getting out and getting here was what she had left and the woman should have appeared and said it's all right now, come. And when she didn't appear the next compulsion drew her.

Jocelyn knew nothing about her, nothing about her before this, nothing about Moriah or Verlia and the one day Elizete slipped and said she knew someone else here — a little vanity overtaking her — someone, Abena, and Jocelyn looked too eager to know more, Elizete stopped. Slipping out. Before she knew it what else would slip out? A woman she loved just so and just so gone? Just so, quick, as if it never happened. This Abena, the only one who could say, no, no, no, it did, she was here, did go, make you sense yourself big and sufficient if you wanted — nothing she did or said but you were waiting for her or perhaps you were waiting for a moment to sense yourself alone. Look, she didn't know any Abena anyway. Verlia knew Abena. Not she. She had only heard the other side of soft abrupt phone calls and long silences after. She had only seen some working in Verlia's head, some arithmetic, stumbled through, long dividing stroked this way, a curving enumerator named Abena. And she had expected Abena magically to arrive, pick up the conversations with Verl, letting her listen in soft-sided and abrupt, tell her, "Vee wrote about you, nice things." But she didn't appear so Elizete saved her name, put it away.

Here you could live just on one street and never know another. You could stay in one spot and never have to see the whole thing. You could walk up and down one street, go to one store, take one bus and never have to see the rest or never want to after a while. The width of the streets devastate you, the concrete-grained deserts high and wide sap your will, the marvel of them withers after nine months on the Jane Street bus. The apartments along the wide street towering out of cement-baked hills were stunning. Here, there were many rooms but no place to live. No place which begins to resemble you, had you put a chair here or thrown a flowered curtain in the window or painted the trim of a door pink or played a burst of calypso music through its air or even burned a spice, a bit of geera or clove perhaps or chadon beni. God knows it needed chadon beni to sooth the ache in your middle. Certainly no room that answered prayer no matter how much rum you offered to the corners nor pious scrubbing with kananga water. There were only places that had a face of their own so terrifying in their muteness, that you hesitated before going in and got swallowed upon entering, without a trace, into their grey persistence. Here no one looked into your face and said "Oh! Is you again," "Aha, where your mother? What she doing now?" No one heard a door slam unaccountably and said, "Is who spirit that?" Here a whiff of the most aggressive perfume could not change the air around you, could not displace that smell of travel which once came like the American dream in suitcases from abroad and which were so seductive, so delicious, so envy filling you wanted to reach out of your skin and say, here, I am like you, here, of course I am not what I appear, I should be where you are, walking casually, casually, in new shoes, there with you, casually in new clothing, laughing charmingly. Here I have run out of my skin. Look here, my voice now without deep sounds or sharp edges or doubt. Here. That smell so compelling that it made you deny your origins, beat back your family, see in their faces only envy of you, only maliciousness, the will to make you suffer like them, drag you down to their hopelessness. Then stiffening yourself against their camaraderie, you begin to speak with an accent to distinguish yourself, affect a tone with disdain in it, hold your behind in like the white girls in magazines, forget things like "good morning," go out rarely but imagine going out somewhere else, in a car perhaps, where the streets glide by and there are lights. Yes, but on this island I am living another life so needlessly, I am being killed, I am wasted. That smell which after all was only impermanence, yours. Foretelling, telling nevertheless, that really, you, would find yourself, cramped, faces as sour as yours, silent, looking out the window, looking away from people just like you and people who made it plain they didn't want to see you either, on the Jane Street bus, plastic bags spilling open, margarine, marshmallows, oil on sale, rice, pepper sauce. Bags spilling embarrassingly, nevertheless goods, goods the mouth needed to taste. For the life of you then, you could not recover that smell. And you thought that you were sloughing off skin over the Atlantic dressing in your real self. Here. Impermanence, which perhaps you felt all along. Perhaps it was built into you long before you came and coming was not so much another place but travelling, a continuation, absently, the ringing in your ears of iron bracelets on stones, the ancient wicked music of chain and the end of the world. Who would know riding on the Jane Street bus, taken up with the present details of eating and sleeping, who could make out the wet brow of people walking out of the sea, who could make out the bridges leading nowhere, the shouts of falling, the gasps of last breaths, who could make out the ripe bellies birthing trouble.

If you live here you notice that nothing ties people together because you notice people don't talk to perfect strangers on a bus going up Jane Street. It's not an old city. Nothing happened here. You can't look at the buildings and say ah! that's where… Things are made up. Not one face here tells you a story, not one face says my mother went blind sewing sleeves, my father dug a mountain in coal, my smile I earned from loving these people and I have the capacity to love whoever I look at. They do not say, I have come back as my great-great-grandmother to finish my life and to eat a leg of pork all by myself; your great-great-cousin was a greedy woman and took all my food from me; salt turned my blood thin and made me weak; I walked up a hill one day and forgot; I killed someone there; when I walked up the hill I was hungry; I am hungry so I have come back. If you live in this city, nobody knows anybody so you could be anybody. If you lived here no one would stare into your face and say that you were somebody's child or look for intention.

Intention. Intention is what she could not make out. She could not get her mind to recognize this place. Jesus, she was making so many mistakes not being here, in her mind. Only her body reacted — ran from the police, ate food when it had to, walked, walked and kept moving. What was this? A room, a station, a clearing, a road. If she could just recognize something it would be all right. She had glimpses. A brightly lit corner, glass walls, lights shining out of a big building. An avenue, a church on one corner, an ornate hotel, lanes of fast traffic. The maze. She liked the places where there were bushes in the front, not the steel fences or the cut grass. A field in a gully, a net with hard wire, a gas station on the top of the gully. At night the gully was dark and the gas station fluorescent. She had never been in a place with so few trees. The subway trains.

She was afraid and excited by the trains. She took them like jumping into cold water, standing under a bucket cascading with cold cold water. One, two, three she heard her voice saying aloud. And missing many before she had the courage to jump in, then the door, quick and hard, afraid she'd catch her hand in it and the light and the silence of the people after she'd screamed like she would scream at home, jumping in the cold water, seeing blood on a cut. Spinning around in the train smiling at her foolishness and the silence there at her turning, closing her smile until she could not stand it and stood waiting to get off at the next stop. And then again the ritual, one, two, three, missing many before she had the courage to jump into another, this time remembering not to scream in the silence of the train.

But she loved the train. The going going of it, the squealing squealing belly of it. And the way no one could get off except where it stopped. Here she began to love whatever held everyone still, like heavy rain or snow storms or bus strikes.

She saw light always bright turned on in the daytime, all day long as if the sky was not enough, on cars, on street lights, in stores on flashing windows, she saw food, every-where and plastic bags in the garbage, food everywhere. So much, so much of everything. She had known that there would be but she did not expect so much. So much, she spent money badly buying lots of toilet paper, and soap, boxes of soap. Matches, saving matches which were for free and plastic bags, white and dense or with signs. Transparent ones for little things. She knew that she couldn't carry it all wherever she had to move to but she couldn't stand the waste so she bought more and more. Piled it into her little room, whichever little room that she would have to flee to and abandon.

After months she still saw no birds to speak of or the same birds, no river to speak of, no mountains to speak of, no grass to speak of, no moon to speak of. Especially no moon. And no ocean or sea. No sound that was the usual sound, no chorus of beetles, crickets, frogs beginning with night, ending with morning. And since this was how she knew the signs of things, she was lost. But she heard the rumble of traffic starting up each day and dying down just before it started again. Just as the city took a breath, at three perhaps four in the morning, she could count the whoosh of a car speeding down a wet street outside her window. A lonely sound, a sound of someone going somewhere without everyone else. Perhaps staring at the road's hush and haunt, perhaps thinking of going nowhere, perhaps longing to be somewhere, the street closing in on them, the car, thin armour from the air outside. And someone in the next room coming home or waking up to leave, the sound of water and the hack of coughing and the weight of the body, legs over the bed, heavy to the floor. This is how she would come to know a place, listening for its four o'clock in the morning.

The noise, the everlasting noise came from nothing she could recognize, no particular machine, just the noise of machinery; but machinery past the individualism of a machine, machines lost from identity. The mouth of them wide open in a yawn. She didn't sleep because of the everlasting noise. She couldn't get used to it. Couldn't sleep for thinking what noise it was, wanting to distinguish it, this is the noise of this, this is the noise of that. Icebox and wire and light-brighter-than-the-moon noise, pitch, crack and the iron haw six o'clock noise of the garbage truck, and the noise nobody makes but the radiator, sighing and knocking in its metal slip.

And the faces that didn't know if she was ill, didn't know that she had a headache, didn't feel or recognize in her face the compulsion of work, the concern for her teeth, the skin around her eyes puffing up. The faces that did not look into her face. "What the hell kind of people is this?"

This is how she would come to know a place but somehow this place resisted knowing. When she tried calling it something, the words would not come. Not easy, not easy at all. Cling to me vine, dust trace walk, water behind me, water in front me bush, take in front track, blind face man, drop me down here fruit. She would not come to know this place no matter how much she walked it, no matter if she set herself to knowing, she could not size it up. It resisted knowing, the words would not come. What could she call a place that could disappear or that did not exist without the help of people? What could she call a place set out so much to please and ease the legs, the heart, the next thought before you thought it, the next need until need was not a word worth saying? This city was imaginary that's all. That's all.

Or was it she who disappeared into her other life, into the descriptions that she had always known and which had followed her here? She had brought herself here with the nameful weight of an island resting against her, at her temples where she remembered and where she collected and where she looked out off. Was it she who disappeared into her life, the tunnels of a wood tunneller, a sand maker, her eyes on the wall her breath held quiet? And each time she tried to get a hold of the city she longed for another place. She did not understand the signs that she should look for. They came hanging like clothes on a line, close, the way clothes are empty and slap wet against the face, stretching from a house to nowhere or at a distance appearing abruptly hung in the air.

The thing was she had no one here. Her names would not do for this place. A place was tangible like a thought. You could lengthen it, fatten it, flailing legs scale it, return to it, greedy, eat it. It smelled of some odour, mixtures, it filled your breath, it was appealing and disgusting. She had no one here, no blood turned thick and cut into edible slabs. This was a place she had no feeling for except the feeling of escape. And not rescue but escape. Rescue would be too much to ask of anywhere. This was the furthest that she could come away from that island and the stone in her hand that wouldn't take in all of her face but dripped and dripped and melted it. She didn't need rescue. She would take a chance on a place with no one she knew. All the places with someone, some relative, some known stranger, all those places had chewed her up so perhaps she had found emptiness enough to fill her up here. Looking for recognizable signs was reflex, habit, just habit. It ran her along the streets and the malls and factories and the rooms and had a good hold of her. She couldn't help looking up and wanting to see water, navy blue and roiling, she couldn't help glancing over and expecting to meet a familiar face or even the face of Isaiah or the face of the woman she was given to.

This was no rescue. Some tangled fight, the room stiff with pain, the times she worried that Isaiah would come back lucid and chop her up.

"I have work here. Nothing is safe."

"Liar," Elizete had told her, clear and undoing. Liar. "You was fine over there. You didn't have to come here. Who the hell ask you to come?" She'll never find out beyond the startling lush who Verlia is; she'll never find out beyond the eyes' deliberate blind.

Verlia had told her and because Verlia was always hurtfully honest, it was true. This was no rescue. Apart from that truth she had left her nothing. Nothing at least that people ever left lovers or wives or husbands. She had only left her the last place she had been before.

"I am not a man," she had said, "I cannot take care of you like that; a man can promise things that will never happen not because he is lying but because they are within his possibilities in the world."

"You think too much Verl. Things is simpler. Why you with me?"

"You know." In her choppy way and hiding.

"I don't know. I know for me. I don't know for you."

And scared herself, unravelling, "I can only promise to be truly naked with you. We'll be very scared walking down a street, hungry all the time, frightened of our own breasts when they meet." Telling it before it harmed her. Not wanting anything round the corner waiting to hurt her. Talking to herself and not to Elizete. On and on as if she hadn't heard.

"Why you with me?"

"I can't promise you..." Quick and stilted, when Elizete wanted her to talk and she couldn't except this way and thinking not another one counting what part of you they wanted, coveting you like goods, wanting something you didn't understand how to give nor felt the need to give it. "Christ, Zete, I don't know what you want. I don't have it."

So she'd ended up in Toronto — had was to leave, had was to run here — living on Jane Street remembering Verlia and how, when there was no answer, she, Elizete, had tried to joke Verlia out of her seriousness, fearful that she had trapped her. God knows Verlia could give big but never small.

"So is catch ass you promising me then?"

Verlia only looked more distressed and she, Elizete, had said, kissing Verlia on her arms, "I already know catch ass, Verlia, you is my grace."

Verlia moved away, refusing her, "I don't want to be. Look Elizete, don't try and seduce me. I don't believe in seduction. If you're coming you come with your head clear. Seduction is a thing between a man and a woman. There is no seduction between women. This is harder."

Seduce? As if she knew the word. She was just being nice, giving her a little sweetness and letting her go. Okay. Yes it was harder she knew but no one could tell her that this wasn't grace. And no maybe it was not just the woman with her back to her now and that frightened sound in her voice, frightened by Elizete's need. Maybe Verlia had simply come at the right time but that was what grace was. Everything changing for good. It was hard to explain this to a woman who had grown up refusing these things as Verlia had. Hard to say, spirits exist and you can call them and they come though of course you must be very careful who you call. Hard to say, who you don't call comes too.

Grace, well this was far from grace and far enough away from Jane Street for her, for the time being, until she could find another room, and someone who knew what happened to her things.

Didn't need to look around though, she knew where she'd land up. She knew that when she opened her eyes a hank of desolate railway would appear, a new doorway at the end of a yard, a factory spitting smoke, a low-down hotel with a bar and a barren clearing. This sureness and ease with ... no, not evil ... did not always comfort her or make it easy. She could not always predict the details of each and every day, its water washing her face. She had only found it so regular and general as to, sometimes if she was open enough, know that it was happening. Well didn't she conjure, boil tampi bush and drink it just to throw herself in the trance of this new dry vision? It appeared anywhere that she landed, anywhere that she came from, anywhere she was going. She'd cut herself against this vision enough times, place after place. And anywhere was better than the place before Verlia. So Verlia think their nakedness was frightening, well she would take that fright any time over what went before.

Seduction. Lies about what was truly to be done to make love. So hard that when it was done she could not call it love, the work of it. Love was too simple and smooth and not a good enough name for it. It was more rough. Coarse like a bolt of crocus sacking full of its load of coconuts or husks for mattress ticking. I lay down on that prickly bed with Verlia after we tease it and pull apart the brown rough flex of living, fluff it up and fill the sack with all of we self and what else we had was to say. What we had was to say wasn't much but it was plenty. For two of we it was the end of a road, she own she write in a arc in the sky and mine, well, it come to grounds. And that is why we do it so furious and so plain. Coarse like the bruise on the back from carrying it and heavy as if you walk into the sea with it and it come out twice the load. I take her for everybody — my mother, the samaan, and Isaiah and the woman they give me to. I want to jump out of the bed and run from she. I had to watch she face good until it return to itself. I wake she up in the night and shake she and ask she to tell me she name and where she come from so I would not mistake she and think the flesh I lay down next to is all I hate. Not simple at all. Tell me what colour was the ground there, where you from, tell me what your mother' face look like, tell me what colour was the stones, but tell me what colour was the ground. And your hand, did you ever want to plunge it in the stones there, did you ever want to battle slate, for it to fall all over your face and your hand beat them into dust, you did see yourself coming out a woman crushing stones. I want to go against the ground, grind it in my teeth, but most I want to plunge my hands in stone. Too simple. Unexpected in the cool of night I would leave her house thinking she possess me against my desire. I would walk all the way back to Moriah and stand there by the junction sweating. And she make things hard, she make me have to say everything, she make me have to tell everything. She want me to open up my head for hell to fly out. What morning I running running, can't find no track, no sense in how, no way out, if I could say, of this body what everybody use for leaving, for toting water, for beating and beating.

I tell she I not no school book with she, I not no report card, I not no exam, I not she big-time people with they damn hypocrisy, she want to dig and probe she could go to hell. She get vex and then after hours the mad woman come laughing and say is true. Salt. It was sea salt and milky like when rain fall. I could not help but think that I was the one who would carry the sack into the sea and out, I was the one ploughing the sand, I was the one going to stay and she was playing because she could leave this island any time. For this I had to find a hatred of she, coarse too and sometime too much. I would sew the sack and stuff it and she would lay down on it. Is so. The woman she have over there, I bring she right in she face. I don't ask you your business, what you have with she and when you done here is me to catch. She face come hard and I want to know that sadness. Not too simple and plain now. She laugh. Nothing to hide she say, nothing is there. But I can't say she ever ask me for any of this and when we in the same room I wonder what catch me. Is a different person that I imagine. Not she. She take nothing, she never do me nothing bad when I really think. When I really catch myself is miss I miss the accustom grieving. Is miss I miss the accustom pain. Them grieving and pain that lay down there for me so to have. I don't feel it. It shock me. I have to be honest she never do nothing bad to me. So when I come to fight she, thinking the whole way there how I just going to argue and fight and who she think she is at all, when I reach hissing like a wave, it just subside.

I wouldn't call nothing that we do love because love too simple. All the soft-legged oil, all the nakedness brushing, all the sup of neck and arms and breasts. All that touching. Nothing simple about it. All that opening like breaking bones.

And in the second place she met Jocelyn from home. From home but you don't trust nobody here so they circled each other for the time being, witnessing and noticing if any kindness was false. Even if weeks went by without revealing any betrayal still they circled and circled, walking softly past each other's door, making sure their dishes were washed and they didn't use each other's toothpaste. It took a while. It was hard to resist the sound of a phrase from home, hard to resist listening to each other suck their teeth when they came home from work. Hard not to laugh when they did it together coming up the stairs. Hard not to exaggerate it loud enough so that the other in the kitchen could hear it and come asking "How things?" Hard not to pour out then. All that took a while and still one could never be sure. So only a little at a time. And still not all. Precarious. If they didn't feel precarious something would be wrong. And at moments when they felt safe from each other, they exchanged stories about how cunning you had to be to live here. If you had to resist friendship what the hell kind of place was this? So in their free time after they'd edged around and made sure, gone past the doors a few times and maybe put on some split-pea soup, a little piece of salt meat and thyme and garlic and onions and a yellow pepper, maybe some singing after the smell rose calling the other one from her room, they would strike up the talk. After some rum and Jocelyn saying, "No, no, no, girl, I don't drink you know…but anyhow I will take a little one."

"You played deaf. You mad or what girl? But that is nothing. One time, you ready, okay, Miryam, the woman I tell you 'bout, who I know, from Brazil. She break she leg jumping out of the window on Tyndall. It was a joke. I don't know, seven, eight of we in the house…. Somebody shout "Immigration!" Rosario, the man I was trying with. One hundred sixty pounds of him and the child new on my belly. All together. My good luck and my ticket out. Look, I lifted him up like it was nothing and it was nothing compared to the fear pumping in my face. "Immigration!" Me and my belly take off. He say he would get me my papers if I let that belly grow. "Immigration!" and it was like the house split in seven, eight…. Nobody care who get trampled, nobody care who get catch. Rosario is the only one with papers. I drop him on the floor and leave him there because he bread buttered, and I run with Miryam. Miryam and me fly out the window the same time. Glass chipping like ice, sticking to we flesh. "Immigration!" What a word. That word could kill, oui. That word could make a woman lay down with she legs wide open and she mind shut. Don't think it en't so. Miryam and me wasn't afraid of the glass. Nah man! What is a window in front of that word. We see clear road. Just a window in front of we? Never. Miryam was asleep anyway so she didn't feel the bone come through the skin when we drop. She keep running until we hear somebody laughing. Joke you know! Well, what to do? Not laugh yourself. We start to laugh and it's the laughing that make Miryam fall down. And if she didn't fall down we would still be running. Glass, broken white bone and tear up skin and me with blood between my legs."

They laughed and laughed and when the laughing stopped there was silence. The room was full of silence, they tried again, the laughing skittered off. A little Ovaltine to wash it down. Then they sighed "Aah well," "Look here now," then the room was full of silence again. Elizete lifted the Ovaltine to her lips. Jocelyn, the memory of blood between her legs, walked to the window. Making a joke of it seemed bearable. The laughter would contain it better, though even laughter was unpredictable. Sometimes it let her drink her Ovaltine after sighing, still hearing the silence in her left ear. Sometimes it let the other, Miryam's friend, walk to the window calmly, the feel of blood between her legs. And sometimes it wouldn't stop until they were wracked with tears. Tears the size of rain. She blew breaths on her Ovaltine, the room was silent. The other, Jocelyn, who had become her guide, turned to the room again wanting more laughter but only finding Miryam's story.

"That girl Miryam, she was from a place named Minhas Gerais in Brazil. She said there was gold there but they never seen any of it, said she mother ran there from Venezuela because a man was looking to kill she, she father worked up there in the mines, said since slavery his people worked in the gold. How you think that girl reach here, Elizete? You wouldn't find me here if I was from a rich place like that. I know how to live."

"Girl, you forgetting her colour."

The laughter skimmed their teeth again, pushed the other to the window again, "Mine too."

Jocelyn pregnant for papers and Miryam in Jocelyn's mouth losing her leg through laughing and she, Elizete, losing her hearing, every part of the body put to use like a hammer or a bucket, every part emptied like a shelf or a doorway.

So much coil and curl, so much fold, hedge, girdle. So much starch and stiff till it's not walk, it's not anything that look like walk or feel like walk. So much so that the body doesn't move any more, don't do nothing called moving, no more oil and sugar, no more girl you can throw that big self around, girl them legs too too fine again, you so sweet honey couldn't describe you, would take shame if it tasted you, 'fact, you make honey dream it was sweet, cane don't make sugar since it find out about you, oil turn to water, water turn to dry land, your hips like a ball-bearing on a wheel, ain't no bump that you can't smooth, ain't no hurt you can't fix. Well, hurt there was now, honey, her face, don't talk about that, the cave of her belly crumbling in a girdle, anything so that she wouldn't move. Call this living. This ain't no living. This is where you do that Black woman trick. Squeeze water from a stone, steel your Black woman self to bear the street, hope for another century, make something that can last another age, something that can wait, for some light.

So I lose my hearing. One day. It was easy. The man call to me with the name I thief, and I so studying the woman I used to be that I didn't hear him. Well I wasn't that used-to-be woman for a good while now but I love she because Verlia love she. Why Verlia love her is not ever plain to me because she coulda love better. Anyway I was like a child for her love. I was greedy for she. So greedy I'm not sure if that cliff wasn't my mouth swallowing Verlia up. I hand her too much of me to take care of. Mind you, Verlia had a love that make she thin. It wasn't for me, it was the revolution. Is the only thing that could make she leap that bounds. Once we was walking in the night near L'Usine St. Marie, the cane boiling smell sweet, sweet, sweet and the breeze playing with the new growth, and just so I hear she say rock-stone cold, "You know how much of our people buried under this field. This place is old as water and since then Black people drown here in their own sweat."

The field gurgle, the smoke from the factory so sweet it stink, my blood crawl from Verlia' certainty. She didn't say anything else and I didn't say nothing neither. That was Verlia' love, the people buried in the field. I was cold beside she, for this love make she feel lonely even as we was each other' company. Verlia would cry watching fields of cane or the stony remains of the sugar mills or the old tamarind tree which someone said was there since then. She understand their witness to them days and when she stand in front of them she was standing in that same time. I see she body curve in pain at these moments, the spirits rush up to hold she in their ache. Under the tamarind tree where they say many get hang, I see she turn transparent and blue in the rain-damp dirt. She had sadness enough for all their sorrow. She remember them in she body. Vein does remember blood. The spirits call she and make their display in she. You don't ever live for yourself there.

En't I had was to get out. Who woulda find me and lock me up? Who woulda kill me when Verlia leave me? I had was to run. I slip down that cliff. I don't know how. I feel stone in my mouth and since stone didn't swallow me as I pray I run. Who woulda keep me now? Quiet, quiet I slip down that cliff and I reach over here.

Anyway I lose my hearing because I think fast fast. This white man in front of me don't know anything about me. What he think already of a Black woman gluing the soles of shoes in his factory? I look square into his white face and it come to me. I put my hand, my left hand, to my ear tapping it. I know it was my left hand because the fingers on it tingle now and my left ear always feel numb after that even when I change factory and no longer had to pretend. I was deaf for three months with that one sign. Never mark yourself when you talk of sickness, never look at the crippled, don't point at affliction, so the woman I grow up with say.

"What the hell you want from me? It's not my goddamned name. You blasted people always want something. I look like any Gloria to you? You ever know any damn Gloria to look like me? You come out of your mother's arsehole or what? Which Gloria you know look like me? Is not my so- and-so name, what the hell you want now? Is not my name. You see any Gloria here? Is not my fucking name, you hear me?"

This happen to me steady steady now. I couldn't point to that ear no more. If I did do it one more time I was going to go totally deaf and what next? Well that finish another work so said.

Her left hand and ear were numb. Her hearing on that side seemed to fail her. She hoped that she wasn't going to lose things like that one by one out of having to make up stories. It seemed so easy because the man was white and because it seemed so easy letting go of parts of herself, freeing in a way to be someone made up every new day, and the joke of it, when she and Jocelyn joked about the trick of it, the intelligence. "Brains" they called it, "Brains" losing parts of themselves, losing reasons to hold on to their physical likeness.

She didn't look like a Gloria if he'd bothered to look. Glorias were skinny with gold ear-rings and rings on their fingers and they smiled more — beautiful smiles — and they wore flowered dresses, they had a lift in their stride, a lightness, and she felt anything but light. Ruby, she didn't look like Ruby either. Rubys were big women, broad and sunny: they laughed, chuckled and had lovers on the side; their arms were wide, Rubys; their hands looked rich and could knead flour and plant zinnias. Joan. Her cheeks were cut higher, more shadow and eyes and she walks as if they need her where she's going. Lonnette, a woman who always has all the news because she presses hair. Lonnettes are stylish with long fingernails and painted despite the work. He wouldn't know a Gloria if he lived two lives. Roses have hard calves and a new scheme every time you meet them, nice people until you get on their wrong side. If she was a Rose he'd really find out. And she wasn't a Justina either. Love men! They just loved men, lived for them. Not men like him though. Justinas love their men Black and sweet no matter what they did, love them thick and with gold round their necks. Do anything for them as long as they bring it home. "Need his fucking eyesight checked taking me for Gloria." Evalina now. A woman who made you take long to say her name and had as many children and long on patience. She would have just looked at him. "He would know if he ever meet Evalina."

No reason at all, unless you call running reason and finding yourself alive, no reason at all she was here except to get out and to be in the last place that Verlia was. Just as she would roll over into Verlia's spot in the bed warm after her getting up to drink water or go to the bathroom or look outside in that nervous way that she had in the middle of the night. No reason for this numbness overtaking her bit by bit or how much of her body she was giving over to the pull of Toronto days. That waking in the dark, and going home in the dark where morning and night were the same and no part of the day governed any more by nature, no sleep that was finished, no waking complete. Truth is she hardly knew where she was. She hoped she would not have to give up any more, but she was losing the reasons for holding on. Like hearing. It was a spur of the moment thing but when she really thought about it maybe she had decided it, contemplated it long and found it useless. If the words were not sweet, if Verlia's tongue was not at the other end of them, then what was the use of hearing? Or speech? If she could not speak to the best thing that ever happened to her, if she could not tell her, "You should wear a skirt, I bet you'd look nice," knowing that Verlia would suck her teeth, stop reading and walk outside, then what was the sense in speaking? And feeling? Touch? How painful if she could not feel or be felt, if the skin could no longer sense Verlia in a field or a room, if her hair did not rise on her back when Verlia was near, and when the tips of her fingers could not touch the stringed muscles in Verlia's thigh. And seeing? The worst of all if every time she opened her eyes she saw a verdant leap, saw her own fingers clutching stones.

She wants to tear them with her teeth, hate is an extra head, another heart. God, she knows, is deaf, male and graceless. A man you don't know bends you against a wall, a wall in a room, your room. He says this is the procedure, he says you have no rights here, he says I can make it easier for you if I want, you could get sent back. His dick searches your womb. He says you girls are all the same, whores, sluts, you'll do anything. His dick is a machete, a knife, all the sharp things found on a kitchen table, all the killing things found in a tool shed. He says don't think about moving, I can find you. He shakes the blood off his knife and leaves. This time they searched her skin, this time they found nothing and took it, too. Elizete, flat against the immense white wall, the continent. She is drawn just so, to navigate, to scarecrow such a surface, immense, flat like the world now drawn just so, to navigate the air, to scarecrow the world, flat like pain, sharp like the world again, her hands feel her mouth, spread-eagled against the immense white wall, the continent. Such a movement, insistent, deeper than will. Why does her body move now, why unpeel itself from the wall, why walk to the sink, why feel her lips, why turn the radio on? The mind cannot hold this killing. She escapes to dancing, she makes a gift of her teeth to chatter, bury it in laughter, say this is the rhythm of the world.

She likes waking, mornings at five, drinking rum, fanning smoke in the damp under the house, seeing rain, women, big rosy ones, walking on her left side, black and turquoise, especially in the ocean, fish for dinner, snapper, bright red snapper, lobster, butter, spinach, beer, shoes, pointed toes, slightly rounded, laced and dangerous, burgundy, whisky, running, candy, toffee, arriving somewhere, moving, the smell of the ground after rain, rain at four in the morning, heavy rain, deluge, things ripped up by wind, orange pop, babash, quick tongues, hands that were not like hers, soft ones, big.

The man had said to her, "Don't worry dear. Just someone to clean the house. I spend so much time at the job I don't have time to do it myself. I'm hardly even there."

She'd thought, fine this is all right, no factory, no boss over your shoulder, not hundreds of people in your business, easy. Don't have to remember any names. When he raped her she thought of sand, her face in the sand, the particles flying down her nostrils into her lungs; she thought of the quarry with sand so thick it caked off like brick. She felt her lungs fill up and stiffen with sand. She felt her breath thicken, dense to sand.

Eva, now that was a woman. She made ackra and bakes, palming the money with the same hand she palmed the wet flour, cut a man from his groin to his throat, late night on the wharf when she was going home with she money tie up under she dress. Next day the ackra taste sweeter than ever and not a one who didn't stop and say how sweet Eva hand was. Marvas dress like man and whistle soft as pie. Missy, always an old woman selling sugar cakes and you never know if she grater it with she false teeth and spit in it before she give you. Dorothy is the kind of woman with a cow foot under she skirt and a pretty pretty face and if she look like she pine after man don't be mistaken, let them come to she house and you never see them again. Is best not to say anything more about any Dorothy. Son of a bitch should pray he never meet a Lorna, they have yards clean clean and sprinkled with holy water and they tie their heads in white and say words nobody else remember and can make you shit your pants and walk backwards your whole life if they so desire. Don't talk about Lorna, she name he better say soft and with neighbour before it. That is who the son of a bitch should try to jack up. She is not a woman to play with, she is not a woman who name you should even say and when you pass by she yard, if you feel she standing there but when you look there is nobody, walk fast. And if you see she face twice in the same day, mark your cards, fix your life, count your days. Irmas love blades — knife blade, cutlass blade, switch blade, razor blade, any blade at all. Them not cunning, just cut your face like butter and stand there and watch it bleed.

Her tongue felt thick and she could not hear. She saw the dust under the couch, the velveteen fabric hanging towards the floor, a raised pattern gold and beige. She saw shoes ox-blood and shine, the door knob far away as if it were not a door but another wall in the room, a button on a wall. If she lifted her head she knew that it would fall off grain by grain and so she lifted it and it fell and crumbled. If she's losing every part of herself then what part feels this, which limb and which sense; whose breath is she breathing with, whose eyes is she using now. Who is in her body making sand, grinding glass. Why does she get up leaving herself on the floor, walk to the sink, recognize her face, turn to it again on the floor, against the wall. She sees paint, yellow paint, the water and blood from her mouth, her mouth stretched from screaming with no sound. When she closes it again it feels wider. She walks out of the house and down the street sure that her sand is spilling spilling all along the way.

She knows that in the house she's just left the man has not moved. He is sitting on the velveteen sofa or perhaps looking at sand out his window. He does not fear her, he knows that she will not tell anyone. He knows that the fingers of her left hand will be numb for some time to come.

They are swollen. Her eyes are bloody, almost closed. There is a bruise near her waist, under a rib. He knows she will not go to a hospital. He knows that she will not go to a police station. She knows that she cannot go back to the sewing factory. She won't tell anyone. Not even Jocelyn. Perhaps she'll move.

They had both lived in this city now, shared its way of making you speechless. Elizete all the way here now husk-like, straying, after she'd lost sight of Verlia and slipped down that cliff and disappeared into here. Back there, when Elizete wanted stories from her, when she wanted to imagine Verlia before she met her, when she wanted to hear the sound of names for where Verlia once lived, Verlia had said that she could not remember all the time she had spent in the city, something had gone wrong with her mind or something had gone wrong with the way she remembered. It was as if the place in her head for memory got paralysed or stood still, the place in her mind which would ordinarily take note or delight went missing. She was never herself after a while she said, her self got shoved down behind her senses, or her sense got pushed back, lowered like water in a glass and she felt airy. After that, years after she arrived, she only felt things as someone watching but not living. Her own voice left her chest. She could not understand the rhythm of the talk around her. Her voice when she heard it seemed far away and there was always a laugh in it as if she were trying to amuse someone or cajole someone into listening to her, or ring out a note, a signal that she was there. She sounded wheedling, small, off-key somehow, beggardly. She'd changed into something like a sidewalk or a box or a pencil or a bit of paper folded in a pocket, she'd lost a way of making herself exist, she'd become useless. She walked as if she'd been pushed out of a door, the way someone squeezes air out of the opening matter of factly while shutting it. And her senses, they were stiff as a pane of glass, she could not be sure of them, she did not know them, they were no longer reliable. At the end of fifteen years, she could not remember the day to day, not even the week in and week out.

Then Verl decided to leave but before she left she'd taken herself for a walk. She'd walked over the viaduct at Bathurst, where the bridge crosses a dry river bed, walked all the way up to Lawrence pounding her hand into the other palm saying, "You will not go crazy, you will not go crazy, you have to remember something, you're going back now — how will you do it?" She was trying to collect herself again, bring her mind back from wherever the pieces had gone skittering. She had deserted herself she knew, given up a continent of voices she knew then for fragmented ones. This one passing by on Vaughan at the traffic lights, nodding, that one bending over at a bus-stop, the air trailing dried out ground provisions, the talk that had become exotic among them all about what they used to do, sing, cherish. There was nowhere that that talk could take them any more, no significance to it except as quaint speech, talk no longer working like broom or shelter; it could not express anything to be taken seriously, not anger not concern, nothing. From the time it had to be explained rather than done, it fell away and they became mute pulling it out for translation, for curiosity, but like a dead language it did not explain them any more, certainly not as they were. Even they found it odd. She'd lived in one pocket of this city among a people eventually accepting themselves as odd. She was not sure that she could live in the world again where there may not be any other motives to interpret, where the language was plain and meant what it said and did what it did. She could not be sure that she need not look for a trick. She was not sure that she could look straight into anyone's eyes. She needed to return more than they needed her there. She knew that. She didn't want to lay this trip on anybody but she really needed to go, to live in more spaces than the breathless little corner she now had. She didn't know if she would recognize any other place to tell the truth or if this city had just about undone her for any other place. She'd certainly done everything she could to hold on to her sanity but in a place where up is down and down is up she wasn't sure that she'd done it. Fifteen years ago she was stronger. Fifteen years ago she had the Movement. Only gradually and before she knew it did the cocoon from which she now tried to untangle herself appear. A cocoon where the sound of life going on was muffled and dreamy. That's what she felt like today. Dreamy and tangled up. It wasn't that she hadn't been busy or working but one action was so disjointed from another, so overpoweringly separate from the other, that she couldn't be sure she was walking along the viaduct at Bathurst feeling stranded on the bridge and wanting to get down on the path below but not wanting to walk and just wanting to go home.

But there was the side of her she had to return to for it; the one missing for years, the one she'd first cut away, then traded away little by little. The one all her fighting made her tired for. She needed fire now. A raging in the throat like water.

Abena could stay if she wanted — Verlia couldn't wait for her. She needed a mission outside of herself. When she didn't have one she was uncertain. She could not be swallowed by any comfort, she could not take that as all. It may be enough for Abena but not for her. This small place getting smaller, down to her and Abena, was stifling and hopeless. Nothing more hopeless than two people down to themselves for company, for air; nothing more hopeless than a room where all the talk is why not and what about me and I feel this and I want that and love me, love me, love me. Nothing more hopeless than a house where some accustomed play-acting had to be done and repeated in every house across cities, forests, ice-caps, continents. Dull language on tongues to lazy to say no and this is not how I'll live, tied to a single human being. I'll abandon air and light if I do; I'll not step out of this universe of duty then. No, she wasn't flesh like that, nothing as hopeless yet.

Old house turned into an office. The street pushed open diagonally from St Clair Avenue. Vaughan Road. At the bottom was a church and a Jamaican restaurant; an ice-cream parlour and a spiritual store took the bend. She should ask there for Abena, the aunt's voice had said on the phone. The voice was older, broken iron in it.

"I can't help you. Verlia's uncle is dead you know. Asthma. Too cold up here. Damp. His heart was swollen. She didn't consider us you know. She had friends in the city. Different kind of people from us. We never heard from her. These new people calling themselves African, doing all sorts of things. She didn't care about us." She paused or stopped to let this come across.

Elizete said nothing except "Oh." Not knowing how to answer this hurt in the aunt but giving it silence for sympathy.

"Well, I have to go. As I said she didn't care for us."

"I'm... Well...you know she had a friend here...no? I have something to give her. You might know?"

"Well, dear, you know some girl named Abena I heard. Well, it's not my business. Her uncle died you know. His heart was swollen."

His heart was swollen, his heart was swollen, his heart was swollen, she didn't care. Ringing all the way to the street the aunt had given her. His heart was swollen, she didn't care.

These alleys like tracks and traces to be short cut through and call messages over. People from home and other places. This is where Verlia must have lived. She must have walked along this road feeling over ripeness in bananas, buying cane from home. She must have been sitting in a room in one of these buildings reading into the night and arguing with some comrade and drinking whisky and being lonely when everyone left or went to sleep because Verlia could never sleep. And at four in the mornings she must have been most lonely and most awake.

There was a record store, she must have lingered here listening to forty-fives of Toots and the Maytels, Sparrow and Aretha Franklin. There was a funeral home and a bus stop, a Chinese takeout and a bakery. This is where Verlia must have been. At the laundromat smoking cigarettes letting them burn down to her fingers. She'd suffer from that when she tried to bend over in a cane field all day. And this spot, stepping here, crossing the street to the office, earlier than everyone and more tired than everyone by ten and drinking the coffees that would keep her awake, thinking of the whisky that wouldn't put her to sleep.

Brick and falling down, a couch plaid and dingy on the porch. The door was open even though it was cold. She hadn't tried to find it when she first came months and months and months ago. Now she stood across the road watching it. She had passed by before, many times before, standing, watching. Some competitive urge that hardly had any conviction in it made her pass by for days, lingering without entering, then going back to the room she shared with Jocelyn and their freezing laughter.

"Ay girl, you must come out with me one night. I have a man sure to get me my landed."

They laughed.

"Don't laugh. He must have a friend for you. Two thousand dollars or less with a discount."

They laughed louder.

If that was to be the end of her she must find this woman. She had come here for something and the something seemed further and further away as long as she stayed tied to work and suffering again. Verlia seemed further and further away the more she was caught up in living day to day, and day to day was over for her long ago though it's easy to slip into them when you're broken down. She must find this woman, tell her whatever it was she had to tell her and then...well. She had no idea about after but there was something she had to tell her.

Abena. She had seen her name on postcards and heard it at the beginning of more and more rare telephone conversations. "A really good comrade," Verlia would say and little more. "Just a really good friend." Or sometimes, "She does a lot of good work." And once, "I couldn't just live in a personal thing.... Not enough." After they would sit, each thinking about what she'd said, and after the phone call or the postcard they would neither of them light the house or cook, but sit in the growing dark until late, each thinking about what it meant. "Not enough." It seemed to be her voice saying it too. Though she was not sure that she fully got Verlia's meaning, what was interesting about Verlia was what she suggested, abandoning the certainty of hardship, not because life had become better but because you recognized its compulsion, that beat beat of it which you did not control and one day you said, not enough, not enough at all. She liked the evening eating them up as they sat thinking, the brooding in it; the words' dark illumination. She liked the threat of them, breaking apart everything she thought steady and even desired but which came apart as not hers at all as soon as these words were said. She liked the always coming apart of Verlia, the always turn of the world, the thought that she had not thought; she liked the way she need not even know this woman who made Verlia say "Not enough."

She had to tell her. Well, if she could form it herself, she wouldn't have anything to tell her. When she saw her she would know. And Abena would know too. Elizete was a woman without a reason to live if she could tell her nothing, without a reason to have come and without a reason to have... She needed to feel the same pain with someone else or the pain would not exist and the reason...

She made so many turns in the street before going in, so caught up in what might happen in the stillness of their recognition that when she entered the door the bustle and noise of languages that she had never heard stopped her. Someone saying, "Up the stairs, turn left." She did not think that she had said anything or asked any question. She could not remember saying her name, her eyes on the full room talking in different languages. She climbed the stairs turning left into another waiting room now of women like her, all from home or somewhere Black.

She watched her, brisk as a broom, her lips gathered over every problem, lines appearing and disappearing in her forehead. And her smile quick to open and quick to close until it was no more than pulling her face over her teeth. And something else, her hands closed into fists most of the time, her cheeks cut from bone only, her body thin and nervous. She saw her work the room like a rake, all the debris scratched clean and tidy.

And she stayed until everyone had left and she was the

last. Everyone dispatched to manage another day in the city, perhaps with pills, with notes, with advice, with appointments, with reminders on how to navigate the streets and the offices and the factories and the hospitals and husbands and boyfriends; how to navigate their wombs and the tempers of the men they lived with and the crying of their children and their evenings before going to bed when they stared at the television and their mornings waking up at four or five and the cold rush of air as they left for a job and the subways and the tiresome walks home and the rage at the doorway once again.

She stayed until the woman wiped her fist over her eyes, sighed from tiredness and saw her.

She was thinking maybe she didn't want to be swept up, cleaned away, maybe she'd better leave before those eyes sought out something to set right and tidy. If she had seen hands big and firm instead of balled into fists, staying would be easier, but it was the fists that made her stay anyhow. Those knots balled up and tight made her curious and tired herself. And relieved. She knew her. And it would be all right to be undone in those fists.

W

The fifteen-seater poised, plunged into the hot bed of La Soufrière, bird instead of plane. The volcanic garden awash in darkness. Unforgettable flowers of mud and molten glowing sang in a carnivorous and mechanical language. Unseen garden, ever and not now. The bodies in the plane yellowed from light, shafts in the impotent sun. Sun never shone a day on this volcanic cultivation. Ornaments of ash and lava, dust-mouth warblers and mud-caked butterflies, garlandage, accompanied the flight. There were pools of coloured air, streams and rivers of vapour. She was dying. For God's sake! She was dying. In trying to get to whatever place was in between — Jesus Christ! — she was dying. And she wanted it. To go with Verlia, to dance the mash potatoes with her in the well of some garden, in La Soufrière's dance hall, on the mourning ground at Guaya, the two of them, their faces in the dried mud hearing some tune or sound or throb from far off, their faces raw and red travelling across, through the leaning coconut, through the red dirt of the mourning floor, travelling to some place away and familiar. She had, there with their faces raw with things past sadness, irrecoverable, slipped into Verlia's skin until she could not tell who had died and whatever she was living and touching was another life and numb to the bone. Mud fish and amazed eye, a bulbous root in the walls. A garrulous flower, a wordsmith of foliage cleared the way with an interminable murmuring. The fifteen-seater plunged into the hot bed of La Soufrière. Bird instead of plane. Mud fish. The sun, turtle's eye, glistened weeping in the darkness.

She fell asleep in the hot face of La Soufrière waking to find herself still alive but in dream, dreaming that she was awake. Sitting in the fifteen-seater on her way to Barbados, the flesh on her thighs tired, gravity pulling it from its bones in an ache. She shook them, massaged them looking out at the shades of clouds. There, two giants on an island, one of them turns and curtsies toward her, standing in that attitude until her window moved out of sight. The plane bulldozed its way through the quarry of cloud. She was asleep, she was awake. Stones filled her mouth and she chewed on them like ice-cubes. Chunks fell into the windows. She did not know the end of the plane and the beginning of the clouds. She was searching. Searching for a mirror to see if anyone could tell that she was eating stones. Down the front of her stomach, there was a thin grey slate with writing on it — something in Spanish or another language. The plane was empty except for the stones and she and a drunken woman staggering past the windows singing, "For the rest of my life…" She could not hear the rest of the song, only saw the face stretching by, undoing itself in cloud. Laying on the stones growing under her back, she tried to settle herself on the grey bits of slate, only the woman who died on her said, "Come on now. Wipe your face, sit upright, walk fast girl, be still, don't gaze. You're keeping me back. You'll fall." And she fell.

Out. The volcano awash in rainlessness, yellowed light and lemurs pacing, lengthening, reaching white arms out of the volcanic garden and a woman escaping, to think and float at the same time, imagining a place to rest. Now awash in darkness, the plane yawning in the molten crater of Soufrière. She could not pull herself awake, did not want to be awake, but to stop understanding that she was asleep. Over St. Vincent she willed the plane to sink like how she'd heard they could into the sulphurous mouth of La Soufrière. She wanted to listen to the mechanical song of the bird, mud bird, plunging into the hot bed of Soufrière, bathing in the glow of its molten yellow, eating hibiscus, drinking lemon-grass oil. She wanted to go off to another life. This one had just about run it down. She did not know why her body kept going, why it insisted on surviving. There, not one hour behind was the island that she had never left, swore to leave to Maracaibo, and not to leave for finishing. She could not imagine leaving. Just the town was far enough away from where she was from. And there, town, she'd only gone when the woman she grew up with collected enough coconut for one cart and stood outside the oil factory from four in the morning to the next afternoon to get it sold. And there, town, she'd only gone to live with Verlia, the woman bursting at the junction. Now she was up in the sky praying for the breath of a volcano, for the pilot to be hypnotized by Soufrière's dull yellow gleam. She didn't want to scream, put me down, put me down. She wanted something cataclysmic, hell wouldn't be sufficient for what she needed. She prayed to Soufrière to open.

She slept a long sleep in the office upstairs at the back. The woman said she could stay there a few days till something came along. She'd suddenly taken her outside on the fire escape and said, "Look I can't tell you this and I'm not telling it to you now but find someone with a health card. You can't be sick here, you can't even have a baby in this country without one. You'll get caught. Just find one and pretend to be her."

She felt quickly cold and motherless following her back along the fire escape. Crazy, without a country.

"Go home, this is not a place for us."

A sound whipping from the woman's throat, muscular and limber, "Look, this is where a white man stabs your Black woman body eleven times and goes back to work the next morning; down east, it happened, calmly."

Bits of paper powdered the desk, "You come home in a coffin, sister, with nobody knowing you were gone or even lived here, your womanness quartered over kitchen, factory, men's dicks..." Newspaper, little pieces fell off her hands,

"No revolution is coming baby, no fine bright morning. No sister, no amen to this. You cannot last, you cannot out-vigil this jumbie, honey. You haven't slept in a year? Well . . ." The stick of a woman in glasses trailed off, "Go home, it's not a place for us."

Go home. And really no country will do. Not any now on the face of the earth when she thought about it. Nothing existed that she could live in. What did this woman know? She know anything about cane, anything about Isaiah, anything about Verlia flying off a cliff?

"Lady, look at my foot, I can't take the field no more and is only field waiting for me."

Why this? Why did she say this? It was so useless. So far away. What they were talking about she did not know. She had not come for help like this. She did not want to talk about the field. It was just that her feet suddenly hurt. It was just that sand filled her mouth. It was just that the woman deserved an answer like this. The woman had not looked at her, she didn't think. Not fully. Not really. She had expected recognition. She had come to say something. Verlia's name. She thought that her face said it. She thought that Abena should know from her face. She wanted something wordless finding them.

The woman sat down, playing with her fingers, not answering but playing. Elizete had to tell her this, she had to tell someone the truth, which was so complicated. She didn't have any answer that anyone besides this woman might understand. Had she ever understood Verlia saying to her "Not enough"? If she had then there might be a chance that she could explain. The woman playing, playing, touching each of her fingers with her thumb, threading her thumb in and out of each. They now sat in the smell of the room, paper and coffee and cigarettes and must and fall, the smell of leaving and remains. And she could not answer her because these were not the questions she had brought here.

"I didn't come here for a life, this is not a life."

She wanted Abena to understand without telling her. She felt that she could or should. That she should have recognized her. She wanted everything to take place without talking.

"Life already take a country and a woman from me."

Didn't she understand? Didn't she hear her say Verlia's name just now, just then? She grabbed the woman's thumb threading and threading, the woman weeping.

"Don't you look at me white. That is what you do with all of them that was here? Don't look at me white."

"It's the wrong place to run."

"Where is the place to run?"

"But why here?"

"It have nowhere else now."

She didn't want to tell her. She wanted her to know without saying, to pick up as if they were in the middle of a conversation. As if she'd run to the line to get clothes out of the rain and then returned finishing a sentence. The conversation they must have had too about what was not enough. She wanted to remember, to be there in that conversation, in that darkness with those words between them blooming, the light going before they knew it, the time of their talking long.

"I used to do this work better, you know."

Something about this woman, Abena, weeping, her way of wording a thing, something about the sound of her on the fire escape, her busyness with her fingers and her lips, reminded Elizete of Verlia that day when the cliff opened like a door, when the water gaped like a furnace. That day opening first with fire, with noise, with sunshine, with Verlia hesitating at the door of the kitchen, her green pants wet with sweat. That day, her face beaded and tight, her eyes dreamy. Something slipping off Abena's fingers and her slippery weeping reminded Elizete of Verlia and that day with everything shining, everything smelling sharp and glistening and Verlia hesitating, waiting for once, hesitating at the door. She'd never seen Verlia's eyes dreamy before, not even when she woke up each morning. There they were now dreamy, dreamy with fear. Her fingers then, now, thrumming metal, Verl hesitating for once but saying, "You don't have to come yet, I'll be back. They need coffee, we're all falling asleep." She did not, had not answered her, just shut the door and gone with her to the cemetery. If she could not go with this woman, whose speed she loved, who was all liquid, whom she took and agreed was her grace, her way of leaping into another life, then she could not live in any way worthwhile. Walking behind her down the little hill she watched the crease of sweat down Verlia's back. She wanted to lick it, she wanted to kiss her neck. She wanted rain to hem them in their room, make the floor damp so they would have to climb into the bed under the window and sleep, sleep until it was over. She wanted it not to be that day. That day, that day they went crazy whirling in the street. The air smelled like smoke, chemical smoke, and she knew that Verlia was not thinking of her but of the other comrades in the cemetery, but she wanted to hold her. Failure always angered Verlia, angry with herself and everyone around. She knew Verl could not look her in the face nor say how she felt. She sensed Verl's body there thinning itself distant, shedding attachment, washing itself in self-hatred, blaming itself, forgetting her. She wanted to hold her, knowing Verlia would think her inattentive to the revolution. They walked quickly, hiding in the hibiscus fences and against the sides of shut doors, leaving the street empty, feeling its watchful emptiness, its danger, its indifference, hot and regular like any day. Their breathing fiery, propelling them quickly towards the cemetery. She took Verlia's hand. It was tense,

[handwritten annotations: "Romantic love story in materiality of politics" and "← force blocks completion of love story"]

wet. Verlia paid no attention. She wanted to hold her but Verlia was gone, somewhere in her head, she knew, blaming herself for everything, thinking life was over, finished. She kept hold of her hand. Something they had been so careful not to do she now did and Verlia accepted wordlessly. They were holding hands, Verlia swimming in her head and Elizete watching, going towards the cadres in the cemetery.

The day was beautiful, the heat dry, every tree in bloom. If flamboyant could be redder it would be blood black. It would have been an ordinary day, a day for going to Grand Anse to swim in its turquoise lap. It would have been that kind of a day if not for the fear and the killing and everything that they believed in coming apart. Instead, in broad daylight, in the cemetery with its whitewashed stones, sat comrades about to die, so frightened they crouched close together, falling asleep amid the hot cackle and noise of disaster. They went in, both of them, the comrades noticing their hands, stirring, then turning away again looking dreamily back at the sky. Everyone dreaming. They passed the coffee around, then crouched in one body against a tomb, waiting. Elizete held her, she knew she was crying, the way that she cried, soundlessly, her heart beating fast, her chest heaving.

She bet all of she life on this revolution. She had no place else to go, no other countries, no other revolution, none of we neither. That day we all went to dreaming, imagining, trying to shoot jet fighters from the skies with shotguns and curses. Who could not taste the salt in their eyes burn a laugh down their spine in a death rattle. We sit down close together in the cemetery weeping. I kiss she back, I try to smell her through the scent of flares. One comrade spin round and round in the cemetery shooting at the sky. We try to calm him down but he keep spinning and running in circles until he fall dizzy to the ground. He eyes was as red as he ban-danna and they was wide open. Somebody else hear MIGs coming to help we. Each hour he would look up saying, "MIGs, yes man, MIGs, I know the Cubans would come."

"They're not coming," Verlia say, "They can't, they're not coming, they can't."

I try to quiet she, tell she he was only saying it for com-fort. I could feel a heat like a fever in she skin. She keep try-ing to convince him until she self fall tired. We all drift in and out of sleep when the Yankees crack the air, crack it wide open with plane and helicopter.

In the lull when there was no bombing they joked. Someone said it's the ones you don't hear that mean you're dead so we must be alive. Verlia kept listening for the one she wouldn't hear as if it could really be a sound, but guessed it would be more than sound — more like liquid in flesh, like cutting meat under water. She wanted to hear that sound if only to take the other sounds away, if only to take the day away and the morning she first heard the planes above, that morning she wished it would rain, but no, peaceful as ever it came, that sound that islands make in the morning grey dust opening, the same as waking up to go to school when she was eight, the same as August in the hills at Nariva, the same as river silt blowing against her dress and her feet in mud, the same as feeling the hot enamel cup against her hands, hot cocoa burning her lips, the same as expecting someone to pass by smelling of tobacco saying "morning" as the first word to another human being, the same as ever, peaceful and smelling of the green well of water named River Mitan. The planes circling, in sounds those mornings had never heard before, yet all the water smelled like any other day, any other morning. She'd thought the sound of bombers would poison the water, make the river boil like hell surging in its belly. She'd thought the morning would not open at all for the sky, would not brighten and call all the day things that flew in it to fly as usual, to sing as usual, to smell as usual; would not silence all the night things to daylight, but it was as if the world divided, people were not joined to it but divided and what they did was inconsequential to the earth, the sky, the river, the air dense with its own business. Not even the earth sided with them and that in the end was unbearable. What did they think they were taking? Only her heart. And take it then, not even that was hers anyway. "We can't own nothing," Tante Emilia used to say, shrugging. "Nothing, Black people can't own nothing. They take it away so till we don't know how to own it." Well, let them take her heart too. If it was so important to some white man thousands of miles away, so important that all these planes were coming for it and all these bombs were going to kill it, let them have it.

Today the sound of bees and cicadas singing tautly tightened the air, as if they were drawing a map of the place, as if they were the only ones left to do it. Their singing thick as electric wires, cicadas, bees singing thick, suspended the island, mapping the few hills, the dried rivers of the dry season, the white river stones, the soft memory of the people who lived here, the desire of rain when it came to wash rickety houses away, or the desire of sun to parch old people's lips, children's throats, the hot need of hillsides to incline so desperately, to inspire weakness in the knees, the cold-blooded heat of noons melting people into houses and under beds. Cicadas, bees, busy with their cartography, their sound like tender glass above, holding these few things, waiting to set them down again, the simple geography of dirt and water, intact, the way only they knew it, holding the name of the place in their voices, screaming so that the war would pass, interminably pass.

Verlia, flying

SHE CAN'T REMEMBER ever sleeping soundly or without fear. Always the door creaks, a dog barks, a frog's well throats inky, a curtain moves in a breath of wind, a tree yields to a breeze, the constant night flute of a *mot mot* hesitates and she thinks someone is out there. Nights pass in long, almond-shaded darkness, waiting. Waiting to grow up, waiting for coconut ice cream, waiting for Sunday to end, waiting for Monday, waiting for crab season, waiting for dry season, waiting for rain, waiting for Mama to make bread, waiting for Mama, waiting for Papa to come penniless from lodge, waiting for fish, waiting for hunger to pass, waiting to grow up so she could buy a whole can of condensed milk, lean it into her mouth and drink it all, and thick wet Demerara sugar, one pound, mix it with Klim milk powder, eat spoonful after spoonful, and five dollars' worth of achar, her mouth reddened, watering from pepper, twelve barra saffroned yellow, sixteen polouri with kuchela, ten fried bakes with cooking butter inside, akra plenty, blue crabs in callaloo, all this when she grows up, leaves these people who do not seem to be able to protect her or themselves or find enough food to eat, and who live so close to the sea that the water comes in under the house, crashes against the pillow trees, is always almost washing the house away, who live near a river that is always swelling, surging over the beach green and angry, whose other shore is always too far away but beckoning, people who do not know what will happen next, who wait for signs and providence and mysteries, these people who say a green grasshopper is a visitor, a brown grasshopper, death, a brown moth, death, a brown lizard, death, who had so many signs for death that looking into each other's faces frightened them. Which made Uncle Randolph so afraid of seeing anyone in the family in case it was a sign of his death, he moved far away into Grand Lagoon and crossed himself walking quickly away when he saw his brothers and sisters, their children and his own grandchildren. He made his wife turn her face to the wall when he lay on top of her to make his children.

She'd go away from these people who could not predict the future even if it were a minute from now or this very second, who could never take care of anything except grief, which they did with pageantry, all the money they could borrow and headlong plunges into the graves of their lost, wailing and fainting into the muddy holes of the dead. They held grief like mouthfuls of cool water, it purified them even though they boasted of its pain, moaned its injustice even though it was due to their own forgetfulness. They arrived at two sticks crossed accidentally in the road and turned back from their destination. One of them walked into the ocean, her dress folded on her head to keep it dry. She was never seen again. Someone said that she told the pelican circling above her "Go tell them I'm drowning." A man had raped her, she had become pregnant and rather than get a licking she'd walked into the ocean. Another made a joiner fool her into twelve years of beatings saying he loved her until she found his other wife and four children living around the corner from her all those years. She left him in a pool of blood with a mark from his eye to his mouth. Brutality she could stand but not betrayal. Another, devoting her life to the study of dreams and apparitions, played *wey wey* everyday, believing in the interpretations of life rather than in life itself, but also in a little self-preservation, each reality pointed to a hidden meaning so she walked on broken bottles, chewed her hair for sustenance, put her fists through windows and ate dirt, for nothing was as it seems. Another had a laugh like sand, hoarse and grainy. She did nothing but laugh since she was a baby which reminded Mama Virginia that she did not come from her womb but from the woman Papa Ti lived with from midday to two in the afternoon every day except Sunday.

Grief they loved, wore it in white lace over cotton and starched collars with bow ties, mauve dresses smoothed over regal behinds and Chantilly hats tipped to the side over ironed hair, black serge over six-foot legs and close-cut brilliantined hair under black number-six headband hats. They loved grief and spent every penny on it and thought it made them holy, they had each a parched well inside their chests, sacred and hungry, they went to funerals of people they did not know, they stood at grave sides looking into the despair of the mourners, their eyes became ashy with passion. They expected peril, listened for it at the window on nights without lamp oil, sat at the open door in the seven o'clock dust and tried to make out its figure loitering or coming, affirming "hmm hmmm" when it moved towards them; they beckoned it, sure that it was lurking, looked for it over their shoulder, their eyes only opened to see it, they stroked it, they prepared for it, laid a place for it at table. They were so vigilant they helped it by making laws they themselves could not live by; they scanned the unformed scars on their cocoa-picking, seine-pulling, cane-cutting, rum-drinking hands; they scanned the scarless flesh of their new born and wrote peril there because peril was all they were familiar with.

They all walked tilting to the left like their Papa Ti, always in danger of falling. Babies became ugly under their kisses. And she, despite trying, caught peril like any disease in childhood, drank it as a newborn. She knew this later when nothing worked out, when she could not tear herself away from hurt, when she could not remember a smooth year, when she could not sleep for the heaviness and trembling in her heart. She had caught it not long after she was born; someone threw her up into the air at three months and forgot to catch her and no one knew that her nose was broken. She remembers hitting the dirt flat on her face, she remembers shock and an urge to get up, walk right out of the yard and leave these people. The one that threw her in the air and forgot began by pretending that he was mad. He hung laundry on the high electric wire to fool the electricity company into letting him go with severance; from then on he himself was not certain of anything — did he really pretend or did he really do it because he thought it was a good idea? He had been the best lineman in the company from the first day he arrived; he liked the height, so above the world he wanted to live there. Another stole mattresses or at least Verlia dreamed this when she had a fever, and stuffed them into the house until there was no more room. A gang of men threatening to kill that one, chased him through the house leaping over his mother and father as if the living-room was the public thoroughfare. After that waiting became unbearable though she was only nine.

So she decided never to sleep again. But to grow up and

go away and to disregard or hide at least the spectres of their movement in her memory. For they existed like spectres, so much shadow and light; she closed them out at the first sign of their corporeality. She remembers in movement an arm rich with flesh descending against her face; faces, dry with madness, strafing the air. She remembers only hints and suggestions, glances of movement, for she stopped looking directly when she realized that looking hard made things affect you. They still did even if she did look hard but this way she forgot. She remembers stillness and anger moving in like weather, hanging, parting the spaces among people, ground and tree, then tightening the air and spending itself till all that was there had no place to go but through her.

She's dreamt the house sailing out to sea, she is in it; she's not sure if it actually happened or if it was a dream — all she knows is that the water was emerald and choppy and many people were trying to pull the house back to shore, that the waves had swept the house away leaving the bleached pillow trees like exclamation points in the sand. That it was raining, that her dress was wet, that her mama Virginia still sat at the window propping sorrow as if nothing was unusual. She's dreamt riding out to sea, a weeping sea, its eyes translucent, its tears glistening, going to someplace so old there's no memory of it. She wonders what tears that old would taste like. She wonders if they taste like stories she wants to hear. But she fears that any mortal self is heavy and persistent, full of presentness, which jostles the air and is unpleasant. She knows that drawing breath is the first mistake; it limits you to feeling your finite body, that empty box with nothing but a greed for air. She'd like to live, exist or be herself in some other place, less confining, less pinned down, less tortuous, less fleshy to tell the truth.

She's dreamt her mouth full of teeth, she's spent her whole dream pulling and pulling, trying to empty it. She's dreamt everyone turned into hummingbirds, digging their beaks into the mud. Their beaks get stuck, their wings beat and beat but still they can't fly out of the mud. She's dreamt this so close to being awake that when she wakes up she swears there's mud in her mouth.

She tells Tante Emilia who reads dreams for *wey wey* playing. Emilia watching her keenly, something like good luck breaking the dreaminess in her face, asks, "You sure of what you dream, Vee?" Then, "That is frog, we must play all the money on number thirteen."

Could it have been as simple as a frog, could her dream with all its drama and what felt like disaster be about nothing but a frog? When the mark busts at one o'clock the number on the tree is thirteen. They win fifty dollars and Verlia becomes famous as a dreamer. "This girl could dream good," Tante Emilia says. Now she dreams for the family. They look at her with respect but with suspicion too, because they do not believe in anything good. The next day she dreams that she is running so fast she cannot see her legs so Tante Emilia plays centipede, then she dreams that she is in the ocean swimming so Tante Emilia plays red fish, then she dreams that she is laughing and they play monkey, then she dreams big fish everywhere and Tante Emilia plays number two, woman and child, and sends all the girl children in the house to the doctor because fish means pregnancy. She is peerless in the competition of dreams, the morning revelations betting on the *wey wey* mark. Ground worm, sick woman, cattle, jackass, jamette woman, morocoy, then she dreamt lots and lots of blood and Emilia played queen for victory, big house, pigeon, shrimp, number twenty-four, number twenty-three, number seventeen and number thirty-two, until she was tired of dreaming. Then she started to have two dreams in one night, then three, then more, and then in the mornings she could not remember them and her mother, shape-shifting out of the liquid of uncles and aunts and cousins boiling in the house and counting on her dreams, said she was wilful and selfish.

"What you mean you tired of dreaming, just as a little luck come to we you tired dreaming, I ever get tired of making you and your sister them. You come out of my belly and you will dream if I say so you hear me Vee. I give you life and I can take it 'way."

Tante Emilia said that too many spirits was talking to Vee at the same time and wrapped her head in aloes and tiger balm and put her to bed. Tante Emilia made her drink chadon beni and razor grass and shining bush grass and threw an egg in water on a Sunday just as the sun came to the horizon, which was the wrong ritual but she decided to try anything to make sense of her niece's dreams again. She suspects that all the village of dreamers have put a light on Verlia. "They've lit a candle, they've paid the obeah woman to sabotage Verlia' dreaming." She's seen them with their two-tongued self running in and out of the obeah woman's yard. Jealousy has confused the night air that Verlia breathes in. Tante Emilia walks around the village throwing words against good friends. After one time is two, she whispers to a neighbour, and the seas and the land shall smite thee like a rod, she sings to her lover, what sweet in goat' mouth does sour in he backside, she calls into the river mouth. Verlia didn't know how to tell her that really she never slept, but fell into dreams when she was tired from listening for the hesitation in the frog's throat, the voice of the breeze against the window, the rain on the galvanize roof stopping, her well of a heart trembling and bursting; that her dreams were fitful, frantic, squeezed into breaths of exhaustion that they were fought for between sleep and caution, that the more exhausted she became the more dreams she had, that she was trying to get away from them, trying to wake up in another place. She didn't want to sleep like them, soundly in the middle of the living-room floor with children walking all over them or in the middle of a conversation, snoring. She didn't sleep because she had to listen, listen for what they never seemed to hear, listen for what they missed, what they did not anticipate, what they blundered into and out of with such damage.

She didn't sleep because she had to watch for their carelessness, the day one of them would steal the last pig and sell it behind all their backs, the day one of them would throw all the cooked food out in the yard in a fury and they would starve, the day one of them would spend all the money on an American shirt, the day one of them would lose the new stove on a bet, the day one of them would get pregnant again and they would all fall on her and beat her, the day they all decided that the children should be given away or sent to the city or have a purge of senna and salts or speak perfect English or stop calling them by their first names or learn to swim, taking them all into the high sea and letting them go. It was carelessness because it was never premeditated or calculated; they simply acted. Sometimes it was a whim; somehow it was always in good faith — they were not evil, they were, yet, deeply pessimistic so nothing worked out. She doesn't know how she turned up in their family; she is their opposite — they are huge, she is small; they are daring, she is timid; they never see, she is watchful; or perhaps she is small because they are huge; she is timid because they are daring; she is watchful because they never see; at any rate she does not sleep and they sleep soundly; she waits and they hurry.

She waits. They taught her that the present was a waiting room, an anxious place on the way to being without them, though they taught her so well that when she was without them, they were all that she could remember. She is always waiting, putting off this thing that should be said now, that thing that should not have gone unanswered. Only to have regret ride her, tighten the orbit of her head, make her taste mustard on her tongue, sharpen her face like stinging nettle leaf. A conversation that she should have had way back then arrives loud and intrusive but with no words just a flush of unhappiness, a discomfort that washes her through and through. She had a permanent buzz in her head, nowhere was happy or the right place, she was always waiting to live, waiting to be without anxiety, waiting to be without them. She knows that none of them remember; they proceed, living their own lives outside of her looking. She envies them. For them, children did not have memories or worries or grief or needs that were more than arbitrary. So they did not see her watching, they did not make out her head swelling with all their languages and secrets. She's spent so much time watching them that her own face startles her whenever she sees it. She walks away quickly from mirrors or she only looks at the rest of her. She looks at the rest of her assiduously if the truth is the point, making sure that nothing is out of shape. She's never satisfied. She's watched them so closely, spent so much time checking their movements that she cannot remember the events of growing up, the thought of them has taken up all the room. When she meets an old friend she cannot remember the name, she cannot recall the jacks they played, the street corners they lingered, the three-thirty dramas after school, who said what about whom, not even the quarrels a familiar face still registers as she waves wildly laughing in recognition but unable to say whether she sees friendship or enmity until the other averts her eyes passing straight.

All the pomerac trees, downs and governor plum stonings, all the mango, lead pencil, copy book, new shoes jealousies have left her. She is innocent. People say she was a tomboy, they say she could dance the mash potatoes and the jerk better than anybody, they say she learned to read at four, she learned to walk early, they say her teeth were strong from cow's milk, they say she was never hungry and a quiet child. They looked in her face to see if she was enough of her father for him to marry her mother, they said she had his colour, they say she was supposed to be a boy but came out a girl. She knows she must have walked home every evening with her friends, she knows that she led a band exploring gullies and canals and back streets and fishing ditches for wabeen and guppies, and running from old men with their flies unbuttoned, their tongues red and pendulous. She knows some evenings she walked all the way home with her head down scouring the ground for pennies, cents, dollars, mixing in prayers and spells — "Our Father which art in heaven, Jingay, Jingay" — planning to buy butter nuts, penny loaf, paradise plums, she knows the velvet texture of pomerac, red on the outside, white on the inside, its taste like a fragrance rather than a fruit, she knows she beat the running Ti Marie trembling close singing, "Mary, Mary close your door, police coming to hold you," she knows she fell, busted her forehead on the back steps one Saturday, she knows the ironed steam of her brown uniform when she runs and runs and runs, she's written her name on the inside of her desk in form two, she dug her initials into the samaan tree in the school yard....

So at seventeen she is standing against a highrise on Rose-
mount Avenue looking up to the seventeenth floor where her
aunt lives. She has never seen a highrise. She wants to take
it in. She does not want to be a never-see-come-see, she
doesn't want to be ungrateful. At the same time once she's
seen it, it quickly goes out of style with her. She's come here
to hurry and awe might take too long. She does not intend
to be a student for ever. After all it is so much building, so
much brick, so much what one might imagine anyway. She
intends to absorb everything quickly. Check them off, hurry
up with what she's come here for. But she is not fully that
person yet. She wants to become some person at the centre
of a life, the bits of her figured out, though she is always
afraid of sinking, as she is afraid of sleeping. She never
sleeps well. She cannot imagine sleeping in the middle of
the night, her mouth open, a well of sleep so deep it takes
over the face. She does not want to think about sleeping
here, she wants to sleep. But she wants to be awake here,
waking into her new life. She has no more time for back

there, she wants it gone. She is imagining Sudbury, but she cannot imagine it because Sudbury is an English name and she is told it is a northern town in the letter from her uncle, and in the letter to the pen-pal she wrote five years ago she said how wonderful it is to write to someone in Calgary, someone who incidentally does not write back, but then she imagines him, gangly and blond with freckles, thinking of her. She used the word wonderful several times in her letter. He is what she imagines. He is the farthest that she can imagine. In Calgary she imagines a farm, wheat, orderly row after row of wheat, the earth yellow and swept, the life far away from where she is from, and she too far away from this life and different. So different, so far away her real life yellowing in the wheat. Far away. So is Sudbury when she arrives. It is baked brown and white but not hot, cold, and there are yellow slag heaps at its mouth as her uncle's car saloons its way into this empty bright town which smells of leather and cellophaned bread.

It is the middle of July. She is overwhelmed by... It actually exists. Overwhelmed. It exists so quickly and all over. Faster, more sudden, more all over than she imagined, more solid than she expected. She feels defeated as one does walking to the point of land jutting out into the sea, expecting to touch the cloud laying next to it only to find more distance, more air as the land never rests against the sky, never leans. The whites are real. She had expected them to

feel like plastic to the touch, like a screen. White. She had
thought that it was a style, a way of living well that perhaps
anyone could acquire. She had seen it on the one television
on her street, against the thick bulb greying into the living-
room, she had stood way back on her toes looking through
the other heads of children, towards the moving black, grey
and white, peering at it. She had admired the showiness. She
had expected to step into it as one steps into a dress.
She had anticipated it, as one anticipates a fresh sheet. She
was about to step into the world, into the thick grey flashing bulb of the world where one acts instead of watches
where one is, is, the sound of 'is' buzzing through her.
Coming here, leaving there was the charm, the first act of all
of her acts. At home they too, left looking at the 'is' of life
on the flashing grey bulb of the television, would imagine
her here, being. They would imagine her doctoring, lawyer-
ing, living in the grey wash of clean streets, apartments,
shoes, purses, styles, walks, snow, coffee. She is not fully here
yet though she thinks that she might have been here already,
she has been waiting to live. She does not expect them to be
really white, really all she's read about or knows. She is still
near the back of the small group of children looking past
their dark heads into the neighbours' window into the face
of the television, she is still propped at her window making
her eyes strong by wishing, reaching them into the living-
room of the people next door, catching only the left side of

the television. She is still in all of the poses, out near the almond tree, red ants climbing her feet, at the door, at the window, leaning out, clinging to the window-sill, her legs dangling, in all of the poses, on her mark, to run away.

In Sudbury all of the people are white except for her aunt and her uncle. She feels a glare, a standing off, a glow around their bodies, her face burns in the grey light. She is not sure that it is the same feeling that she had anticipated, but she feels out there, in the centre. And at the airport in Toronto she had felt that way. Important, at the centre of the screen, her hair permed for the first time, her leatherette suit, her silky shirt. She had assumed a cinematic distance. And it had lasted well into the second day because she had arrived at night. The lights of the city lensed her entrance, the drive along the highway, the clean streets, the odd white couple on the corners of this-and-that street, everything in its place as it should be in the world of a movie's world, the dark but surely manicured park with the pond at its edge, the conveniences, nothing needing a search for a paper bag or old newspaper, nothing muddy and needing a sidewalk. Her aunt picks her up at the airport and drives her through the city. She knows that her aunt wants to get rid of her before she gets the idea to stay, before she becomes a liability, and the drive from the airport is full of "When your uncle comes to pick you up," and "You'll like Sudbury." The aunt does not bother to name any landmarks. She won't be needing them since she's heading for Sudbury. She is grateful that family does not cling here, it can't. Her aunt is thinking that she doesn't want another mouth to feed, her aunt is thinking that she has to get up in the morning at five and go to her hospital job and she doesn't want someone slow under foot, she doesn't want to teach another country-boukie-come-to-town, she doesn't want to teach the shuffled footwork, the rhythm without music of getting up and going to work. Well, it doesn't matter, her aunt needn't worry. She is already in love with this city. She is already living here, she has been waiting to live here. She will manage even if it suddenly scares her. She will not be timid. They speed through the west end of the city, sleek and dark, the lights a long fluorescence through the speed, the highlighted shine of a car's hip, its flank, its glass. She likes the dark here, it is rapped in light, it glows, it crackles, it appears on the curve, black, slipping, skimming, light.

Laurentian Leather Goods, the first sign she reads in Sudbury. Driving in the long long sleepy drive her uncle talks all the way through, she half sleeps afraid that he will find her unmannerly or not fit to be with until she hears the sound of an iron vault closing. They must be hundreds of miles down an iron road. Driving in she feels lonelier and lonelier and out of sorts, different from how she had planned to feel. This was not the middle of the world. Where she had planned to be. It is an iron road. She feels the taste of rust in her mouth, the thickness of rock. She tries to shake herself awake as the sound of the iron vault echoes in her half sleep. What is it, the road gridded iron and the wall of baked rock hardening.

Her uncle's kitchen is sterile which is the next place that she remembers apart from the streets which are icy but there is no ice yet. There is no ice yet. She has never seen the ice that she is thinking of but it is the ice she thinks of here. Ice is all she can associate with this place. It hits her in the kitchen in a cool wave. That short precise opaque word, ice. Ice. It is only one word. There is no breaking it. No matter how many times it is said it is still impenetrable and inde-scribable. Her uncle and his wife tell her of all the oppor-tunities waiting. She must choose something do-able, a profession which will help her to earn a living. Not some-thing unreasonable. Something to make her a nice little living. Physiotherapy. Wasn't she thinking of physiotherapy? His wife smiles. And his wife's smile is red, lipsticked and Vee knows that his wife wants to love her because her uncle loves her and his wife imagines, as soon as she greets her at the door and says that she is Auntie Idrisse, that she is the child that they cannot have and Vee feels a violent hunger in Auntie Idrisse's trembling hand. Her uncle's face says it too, though it is serious in his serious way, closed in case of dis-appointment, closed in his hunger for order. She cannot blame him, she needs order too but the kitchen is hard with hunger. Hers to start her new life. Hers to do away with this kitchen and this aunt and this uncle as soon as she enters. Theirs to make the kitchen and the town complete with her adolescence, perhaps her laughing, her adoption as their child, they need her for perfection, acceptability. Even though the adoption was just for the immigration and she is past adopting. They need her. They need a child. Though she is not a child but their imagination can see 'child' in her skinny body, her expectant eyes. She has not yet weaned her face of milky expectancy. She hasn't yet wracked her body on Scotch. They need to fill out the little picture even if it is not a picture of them, but it is a picture to put on the cabinet, as pictures are, to assure them that what's roiling inside them won't jump out, is held back in the frame as they held their breath at the moment the shutter of light opened and closed. They came to this town together, to get away and to find work. They had heard that teachers, yes teachers and nurses, were a shortage in Sudbury. So they had come to get away and to find work where there was scarcity. Teacher and nurse, they had hoped to come to Sudbury and get away from it. They want to be ordinary in an unordinary world. They saw a chance in the news passed word of mouth from someone else who had gone to Sudbury, heard as they hear, listening for advice on how to blend and make it, they ignored any nagging feeling, any opinion saying it would all be the same. They wanted to strive, not like some who would be held back by malice. Malice is what kept them back in Toronto; friends who ached on all day and all night about how hard it was. "These people," her uncle would say, "don't bother with them. Anybody can make it in this country. Is a new country, it have plenty opportunity. Don't let nobody tell you different." So they went to Sudbury, fed up with the malice and friends who wanted to keep them down. Her uncle wanted nothing negative, he said, in his life again. "Nobody can't treat you bad," he said. "Is up to you, in your mind, to know who you is. People can't treat you bad. Is only your mind can think that. You just like white people. It have no difference. Is in your own mind."

In Sudbury, if they conform to some part of the puzzle, they are convinced that they will be rewarded with acceptance. Ordinariness. Man, woman, husband, wife, couple, parents, Black. They are counting on the first six words. They think that her addition will fill out some of the rest somehow, she senses, make them white in this white town. She senses a bargain here. The trembling violence of Aunt Idrisse's hands gives it away. They are lying to her; she is supposed to lie back and then lie every morning when she wakes up, dresses, pretends that they are going out into this town peaceably and unafraid. Preparing to take nods at their unspoken Blackness, smile deferentially and disprove every day, by their quietness, the town's judgement on their blackened souls. When they arrived this judgement had confronted them and now they were filling her in. It does not matter that in this white town, they will remain odd, they will never be noticed as fully there. They are imaginary. They have come as far north as they could imagine. And they have imagined themselves into the white town's imagining. They have come here to get away from Black people, to show white people that they are harmless, just like them. This lie will kill them. Swell her uncle's heart. Wrought the iron in Aunt Idrisse's voice. They are saying, "Look, it is easy — you can imagine yourself out of your skin and no one will notice. It's only if you make yourself visible. If you blend in and mix there is no problem. Don't bring any of that Blackness here, we're ordinary people, we have to convince them that we're ordinary. You can't blame them for thinking about us that way. Most Black people don't know what to do with opportunity."

"It's out there eh girl, it's out there. I don't want to hear no excuses. Look, you have a roof over your head, it have food in the fridge, all you have to do is take the opportunity. Auntie Idrisse will get you a little job in the hospital, that is for your own money." Her uncle says this turning from welcoming to brusque, turning away from her and the uncle she thought that she knew. People abandon each other she knows under certain circumstances. They look away when they cannot say what to do any more with certainty.

How is it that his face is like his father's now? A man he

never passed a word to, a man he thought he was growing against, a man he did not want to favour. How she is stuck in these moments in her family's life, even this far away. In this kitchen, the farthest away that her uncle could imagine, his father has come with him, riding in his cheek-bones. She sees him there, Papa Ti, in her uncle's face, in the cave of his jaw. He had two outside women up until his death. They came to his funeral. One was as old as he, seventy-five, the other was young, forty. By the time of his death he was quite lonely. He was old. Most of his friends had died and he had stumbled from their wakes, his gone eye watering, stood at their funerals, sung in his hoarse off-key voice to their friendship. He had worked himself to the bone. Shot himself in the foot. To prove he was a good servant to a white man happily dreaming of slavery. He was tall, thin as a stick. He walked with his head in the air, shaved his face every day, made daily notes in his diary. He wore white shirts which were ironed stiff and kept in the wardrobe in camphor. His walking drifted to the left. This was because he was blind in the left eye. He was a good man, that's what they said at his funeral. Her uncle did not go to the funeral. He had promised not to shed a tear for this man who had hurt his mother. He had promised to stay in that country only until the day his mother died. He had spent silent evenings with her waiting for his father to come home. He never had a woman, even though his mother told him to go out and meet a nice girl; he waited with his mother for his father to come home. They were both quiet when the father came home, then her uncle left, passing the father without a word. When they moved to town, the father didn't come and her uncle and her grandmother still sat together eating or talking, he watching over her and waiting.

Vee only remembers that her grandfather brought paradise plums and dinner mints and turtle eggs and thyme and chives and dasheen and yams and news whenever he came, and two days after he arrived, after the news wore off or the food was eaten away he became quarrelsome and unbearable and they prayed that he would leave because he wanted to make fancy new rules about children's behaviour and began to criticize Mama so he had to go. And it was really sad to see him go the way he had to go. He probably wanted to embrace Mama but he'd done too much damage by then. So he dressed in his white shirt and fussed over shaving and the children shined his shoes until he was satisfied and then he lingered until the last minute and then he walked away. She remembers his head going up the street above the hibiscus — it was square and balanced on his thin neck and he held it higher than his six feet. He had a moustache of grey and white bristles and his gone eye sometimes cried. Particularly then. He is the only man she's ever kissed with genuine love. She hated going to church with him, because he would sing louder than anyone else and out of tune. He was a lay reader in the church. He missed Mama when she went to town and after she died. She was his link with his family. She died not thinking of him at all but of the sea in Toco, the purple of the island where she was born out at its horizon. She died hoping to forget him. He was the only child of his mother and father. His aunt never touched meat he said, and whenever she came to visit from Montserrat, he bought a new pot to cook her food and a plate and spoon. This is what he told his children. This is what she remembers. Of his two women, Mirelda and Irene, Irene had a sore foot like his. Sore-foot Irene, Mama Virginia called her as if she did not smell the sulphur thiosal from the foot of her own bed at night. Their sores must have bonded them. Lifelong and visible signs of a wound much older. Sore-foot Irene and Papa. God had given them something to take care of and to bear forever. Theirs were the incurable sores near their ankles, bad blood. Hers is insomnia.

She cannot sleep when nights come. Perhaps she has a wound like Papa that she is only beginning to discover the source of; he must have found it. He must have felt it walking away like that, unable to say a tender word or have himself understood. It was all those years of holding water in his mouth for that white man that he could not empty it even for his intimates. Everyone there had something that they could not recover from, something crippling, something that scarred them. She has her insomnia. Hers is not

visible like Papa's sore foot and could be mistaken for something ordinary, something that millions of people have for
some ordinary chemical reason just like Papa's foot could be
due to the bullet that he shot into it or his slight deafness
could be due to the marble he stuck into his ear as a child
when he was so fearful of telling his mother that he waited
until, luckily, he sneezed. Then all of this seems ordinary,
something chemical, some childhood mischief, like Papa's
ear, some personal miscalculation, like his foot and the gun.
But something of it seems hidden or preordained. It could
have been that one night she had a nightmare and the next
night she became too frightened to sleep though she could
not remember the nightmare and this continued for the rest
of her life. But for some odd reason she was unable to shake
the frightened feeling, and after that she felt pointed out,
out of her self and always visible as if she could not walk
about any more without being noticed. Although she could
not remember the nightmare, it lay over her like a skin, so
much so that her eyes ceased to feel open and there was a
feeling of a weighty arm around her shoulders. All of her
movements seemed delayed or not hers and she had the feeling that all of them — her family and the people who lived
all around — were also moving in this nightmare with these
arms around them and though hers was insomnia and theirs
a sore foot or the urge to chew the *passée* of coconut con-
stantly or walking with a limp when nothing was wounded

or the inability to keep a job or not being able to stay out of jail, they all, these movements, these hurts, had the same look to them. All of them had something they could not remember but made excuses for. Their bodies and the acts they committed everyday fell into this attitude, this night-mare, so frequently and intensely, they forgot even longing to be awake. Sometimes she would wake up with a need to taste sugar and before she climbed out of the bed she would resent them, there in that place that she came from and that she hated. She hates it in the blood, it tastes like saliva, sweet at the bottom of her tongue. It makes her mouth spring water, yet she cannot understand why really, only as if she was born into it, like cutting yourself because you are cut or hanging yourself because you fell down a cliff, as if drink-ing poison will ease poisoning.

She wants to run. She does not want to climb into grief any more, the grief waiting for her in their tumbling tum-bling life. The grief that does not end or begin and is wide wide and haunts. She wants to run. Who does she have cut into her face, whose brace strapped over her mouth, who inside her will jump from her any minute and take this bar-gain that her uncle offers her. Take this, it is enough for you, it's all that we can get, it is more than we can ever have. This bargain like the one he had made to sit next to his mother until she died. And she finds nothing wrong with this except a life passing, except a life shrinking in its smallest place.

Nothing wrong with this love except it adds nothing and love like this is too small for her. "We lucky to be in Canada," her uncle says. "You could do anything here." Anything, anything he keeps saying but his anything is small. He means there will be no hunger, you will have clothes on your back, you will have shoes on your feet, and that is enough.

She has nothing to say, she cannot explain it. She knows that she will sound childish. She understands the cast of their faces, she can sense it in their eyes; there is something there that they veil even though you can see that it is hurtful. But they can't admit it; it would give them grief. She can hear it, the way their words end neatly like a tied-up package. She smiles, only half insincerely, signing the bargain but she cannot wait to leave their presence. She wishes that they would show her the bedroom they promised. She's never had her own bedroom. She feels heavy in their love and nervous. If this is love. She knows that they think it is. She senses it, too easy, too eager love and she senses that it will quickly evaporate or turn sour if she angers them, but for now they want it and she wants to leave the kitchen with its veneered cupboards, its clean electric range and too full fridge. Its smell of donuts. Donuts, donuts is how Sudbury smells and food wrapped up and frozen. She is wounded, sated, in the kitchen stuffed with food, and wounded. She cannot see how they think that this is love, how they think that she should live with them quietly dying in acceptance, asking permission and begging pardon, cutting herself off from any growing, solidifying when she wants to liquefy, to make fluid, grow into her Black self. She cannot see how they think that this is love. They must have decided to cut themselves out in this way to avoid the trouble of their skin. But how did they make the leap into thinking that anyone would buy it? They must have seen love on television. She cannot speak to her uncle anymore. He wants a conspiracy. His voice is now chummy where she remembers it as imperious. When did he stop carving ebony heads, like his, varnishing and polishing Ibo cheekbones in the cast of his own, bending over in seriousness. When did he stop beating copper into masks he knew he remembered could speak, sweating over the stone and hammer, days on end. He now says we will keep our Blackness a secret and of course I need your cooperation. He's become obsequious, and she doesn't like the new weakness in his face as if his eyes lifting from his copper work long ago saw something that make him drop his tools. All of this makes her as uneasy as the house back home full of disaffection. Well, all well and good for him, but she can't understand why they would want her to live this way. Why they wouldn't say, "Ay look Vee, we're dead, go enjoy yourself." Instead they were offering her a pillow in their grave, in their coffin engraved in ice, ice, ice, in their donut smelling walking dead sepulchral ice. Instead they're saying yes, they're right, be who they want you to be, tighten your stride, be as thin as burnt paper, taste dust, you're a nigger, be a good nigger, serve, find some nondescript white people, these here in Sudbury are as good as any, and genuflect. Her uncle's laugh is hacking and asthmatic. The cold is not good for him.

She wants to go back to the highrise falling on her three weeks ago, her leatherette suit with its too narrow shoulders stiff on her body. Her body feels prepared, fit for North America, slick. Then she felt as if at least she had a chance standing under the tumbling highrise, but in her uncle's house full of food she feels broken. She'll grow the perm out of her hair. She's been waiting for this. She'll grow it wide like a moon. She does not want to be harmless. She does not want to be a physiotherapist married to another physiotherapist or to a tool-and-die maker or a computer analyst or a sociologist, or to the dry skinny Black man she expects her uncle to bring home, because she is only half the person she expects to be and she might fall for it. She is as much in danger of accepting the perfect picture as her uncle. Yes, the college to study physiotherapy and then the skinny Black man and the house on a street in Sudbury where there are no trees, but the slag heap when she lifts her eyes and a paved driveway that she crosses in white stockings, and a white floral mist when she opens the front door. She is terrified at this seduction. She talks to her uncle less and less. There is less and less to talk about. She had hoped to talk to him about the Movement but he sucked his teeth the first time she asked and said "A bunch of skylarkers."

She cries for three weeks in the room they've given her. She hears them talking but cannot make out the words, only that they are arguing. Many times they said nothing. She comes out of the room less and less and Auntie Idrisse thinks that she is lazy, doesn't want to get-up-and-get in this white man's country. Well, you're making a mistake if your uncle's family think that they can just dump worthless people on us. Vee slips into childishness, crying and not answering when they call. She cries rain, throws up and locks the door for three weeks. When the swelling of her tears doesn't go down, she is on a Greyhound bus to Toronto.

She likes the way the city never goes to sleep, the light never leaves, she has company all night long. She listens to the coming and the going and it is all one, the night doesn't leave, the day doesn't begin. Someone comes home next door and someone leaves. Time is tended to. There is no moment when something happens and someone does not know. She stays awake now just in case something happens. She doesn't want to be left out of anything, not the knock down the hall nor the footsteps past her door. She hears everything, voices on the second floor, the woman with the not-allowed child across the hall. She listens to the news from everywhere on a short-wave radio. To tell the truth, though she'd promised not to miss anything, she misses the news on the radio, the BBC at four and "Rolling Home" till six. So on the short wave in her apartment on the third floor late at night she listens, feels the line ridges of the dial against her fingers, hears the waves stationing, boiling to a place in the world she wants to hear from, in Spanish, in German, in Cantonese; she listens to Radio Havana in its earnestness, to Radio Moscow, its English, stilted, fatherly. She remembers there mostly now, how she felt like walking away when everyone was asleep, how she felt so ready, the waves of another life blowing through her, how she heard a sound waiting for her at the end of sound, how the nights there were so quiet, so quiet she heard a sound waiting for her at the end, how she heard absence, how alone she felt, how like heading out the door. It makes her leave the radio playing, filling up the air where even the ongoing sound of this city leaves open air. She falls asleep like this but only after she hears the world moving again. Someone next door getting up to go to work. The light of morning coming through the kitchen. She falls asleep at the desk or on the floor, a book dangling, the radio fading in and out, the light coming. It is as if she does not trust the world to continue without some tending, without her listening, without her eyes open, without her watching. She sleeps when she is sure that someone else is awake. She falls asleep now when she is sure that nothing will happen without her. She falls asleep to the radio crinkling and shushing. In this city, big as it is, such as it is, she can finally sleep. She feels safe, such as it is. There are so many lives being lived, such difference she is sure that her singular one will not determine the make of the day. She has left forever one village, one town where the spirits seemed set only on the people she was born to. They do not have to wait for God to send rain here, or money, or punishment. Unsettled spirits do not roam the roads, each baby born does not have to be protected with black beads. Here they could not find her — not her family and not the spirits. She loves this city and the moment the Greyhound bus set her down on Bay Street. She knows that this city will not disappoint her because she expects nothing; only what she can make. It is raining that morning, the bus had left at midnight for Toronto and she'd stayed awake all the way or at least she can't remember sleeping. All the nerves in her body were ready for some great thing. The city is wiped in grey light, she hears a streetcar's iron shoes, feels the dampness of a morning she has been waiting for. She walks outside the terminal, by the taxis sleeping on the corner, her knapsack on her thin back. This is the city where she will be. Her legs are shaky, her teeth chattering even though it is not cold. She should wait for her aunt but instead she begins to walk along the street with the iron rails for streetcars and then south on Yonge Street all the way until the railroad, then north again to Bloor Street and left all the way as the light brightens more and more into morning and she sees the city waken, a garbage truck first then a car then two then she stops counting, then, crisply, people going to work. She says good morning to several people and is ignored and finally stops. Too many people to say good morning to or look into their faces for familiarity; what is custom where she comes from is strange here. She must learn quickly. She walks all day, following streets to other streets, to alleys, to subways, to parking lots, to shops, to garages. There is the smell of burning hot dogs in the air and the odour of a city new to her. She follows people, looking for the first brother, the first sister. She must ask where the Movement is. If she can find a street where her people are she can find a room, find a way.

She's left them anyway, the two standing waving her goodbye at the bus station in Sudbury, the aunt ready with new instructions looking for her at the bus terminal on Bay Street. And all the rest back home. Now she will try to remember the in between. What she did as a child while watching them, what she forgot, what she could not remember for remembering the things they forgot, for guarding their carelessness. What she wanted to be.

She finds a room in a house on a street off Bathurst. She chooses this street because of the barber shops on Bathurst. It is Sunday but she knows that on Monday this is where she will meet the sisters and brothers in the Movement. This is where she will cut her perm, this is where she will begin. This is where she will grow thinner with whisky and talk and work for the struggle. In the room she locks the door, she places her knapsack down and looks at the empty floor. She loves it. She thinks it spacious. She has a large window facing the street and she can hear the cars going by. She'll sleep here under the window so that she can always hear the drone of cars, the noise of her city. She'll never furnish this room, a place to sleep perhaps, a table to eat from but nothing else. She wants it bare, everything bare. No photographs, no sentiment, no memory. Everything down to the bone, everything she thinks, now bone sharp and clean. She doesn't have to keep any secrets, she doesn't need to watch for fury, she'll dream and it will mean nothing. She sits there on the floor in her first room for a long long time.

[handwritten: Radical political character, resistant energy, Venia symbolically represents these feelings]

She wants to be the kind of Black girl that is dangerous. Big-mouthed and dangerous. That's what she came here for. Telling it like it is. Yes get your honky ass out of my face! Who you white people think you are? Who the hell you're looking at oppressor muthafucker?

"But you see, but you see, me knowing me, Black proud and determined to be free could plainly see my enemy...."

[handwritten: Allusion]

"Decolonisation is always a violent phenomenon.... It is willed, called for, demanded ... in the consciousness and in the lives of the men and women who are colonised.... This change is equally experienced in the form of a terrifying future in the consciousness of another 'species' of men and women: the colonisers."

[handwritten: Radical scholar to leave this period]

Terrifying future, muthafucker. Don't even look at me. Prepared for struggle, prepared for struggle. She is weak with the beauty of these words. They wash every moment of

157

fear away. Before them there were no words. Ready for the struggle. Ready, yes, to take on the pigs.

She wants to take a photograph in bell-bottom jeans and a green dashiki. Her hair fills the subway door at Bathurst and Bloor. And there's a way that she walks, a way her Afro demands, straight up, Black power straight up. When she walks into the train nobody white dares look at her, too much wickedness to look, too much to account for; they have some vindication to do, repentance. All of them kill all those people in Vietnam, kill Lumumba, going to kill George Jackson. Nobody here can claim innocence and don't lie. That's the righteous truth. If they don't feel the weight of their history, well, just take them longer to be human. Don't have time to save no white people, Martin Luther King tried to do that. In another photograph she wears plaid bell-bottoms and the Cuban flag on her chest, she is laughing, walking across a park with other brothers and sisters. In the Movement. She's come into some real love here. How did she fall into that sweetness. Look at us laughing into the park. Henson-Garvey Park, we named it, right here in Toronto. Look at us laughing into this new name and into our new selves. She's come into a generous thing when she can walk into a park and have people greet her: "What's happening, sister", "Power to the people, sister", "A salaam alaikum, sister". In the struggle for liberation "Individualism is the first to disappear." Fanon said: "The colonialist bourgeoisie had hammered into the native's mind the idea of a society of individuals where each person shut himself up in his own subjectivity, and whose only wealth is individual thought.... Brother, sister, friend — these are words outlawed...because for them my brother is my purse, my friend is part of my scheme for getting on."

She knew that it was possible to leap, it had to be, out of the compulsion of things as they are or things as you might have met them. She knew that there had to be a way out that wasn't succumbing to apparitions or accepting one's fate. She wants to be awake. She had to get out of where she was to understand it like this. And it doesn't matter that it's Toronto or a country named Canada. Right now that is incidental, and this city and this country will have to fit themselves into her dream. It could have been any city, London, Glasgow, New York, Tulsa. If, at the moment that she turned seventeen, they had been where she was sent on the family's five-hundred dollars and told to make something of herself she would have left, ran happily away to find the Movement. If they had been the next runway for plane loads of cheap labour, the next landfall for miserable human cargo she would have been there or longing to be there. Any city would have done it, any city away from the earth-bound stillness of her own small town, any city from which she could look back from a distance separating her own being from its everyday pull. Any city where she could be new. Any city where she could start out. Any city which could banish dreams. Any city gouging on the raw raw science of streetcars, skyscrapers, no family, no grief. If at the moment that she turned seventeen she had read Nikki then she couldn't help it. *Same w/ Elizette, does not have Franklin to relive Adela's tragic ending*

"Aretha doesn't have to relive Billie Holiday's life doesn't/ have/ to relive Dinah Washington's death but who will/ stop the pattern..." Regarding sadness she too can leave. She doesn't have to relive anybody's life either. She at seventeen could deliberately misunderstand her family saying go make something of yourself. And think perhaps they wanted her to go read Fanon and Nikki. "I want to write/ a poem/ that rhymes/ but revolution doesn't lend/ itself to bebopping". Go sit into the early morning plotting your salvation, she could read them as saying; study Che, Ho Chi Minh, "the pitfalls of national consciousness," give Marx the only chance you'll give a white man, learn guerrilla tactics from Mao. These being the things that she needed to know to make something of herself if at seventeen she has a collection of clippings in a shoe box under her bed, one of Chairman Mao Zedong smiling into his mole in Yenan, one of Nina Simone in concert, one of Adam Clayton Powell preaching in New York, one of Ghandi, his glasses glaring, his hands cupped, one of Rosa Parks looking small, one of a lynching in the south, one of Fidel with "Fidel!"

written over the top, one of the Black Panthers, armed on the steps of a courthouse, one of a letter she'd sent to the editor of the island newspaper under an assumed name saying that the student protest at her high school was not futile and juvenile delinquency, as the paper had asserted, but a protest for the freedom to wear Afros and to be natural and have Black pride; one of James Brown in concert, one of Cassius Clay with "I'm too pretty" underneath, one of the Supremes, one of Otis Redding, one of Uriah Buzz Butler, one of a drawing of Dessalines at Cap-Haïtien. She's been collecting bits of newspaper ever since she saw the face of Fidel with "Fidel!" written over it when she was seven. He looked to be looking right at her and she'd never seen such joy before. And her uncle and everyone around kept shaking their heads and chuckling "Fidel, man!" and they drank rum at the rum shop listening to the radio and shouted, "Bust they arse Fidel! Run them out!" And after drinking at the rum shop the uncle who no longer wanted to see his family took over the town hall in the name of Fidel.

Then she'd started to collect each time that feeling came. She started to collect faces illuminated in some great event. But more, events which seemed to galvanize the town that she was from. If only for a moment or a fortnight at the most, they'd spring to life in the glow of these clippings or in rumours of some set of coloured people somewhere beating some colonial power down.

She would have taken her shoe box to any city at seventeen. She had been waiting her turn to leave, waiting after the aunt and uncles and the sister settled, reading the letters about moving to Hamilton, about moving from Hamilton, about better jobs, about the country opening up, and about the ticket and at least two-hundred dollars' affidavit to the back of the passport to tide her over, and about Sudbury. She had been waiting to turn seventeen. A burning waiting which had taken up the whole year with eavesdropping on conversations and secretly reading letters from Canada. And alternately trying to behave so that it would not be taken away and misbehaving so they would have even more reason to send her. If at seventeen she deliberately misunderstood some careless direction, she could not help it. She had been preparing too long, plotting this misunderstanding too long. If she misunderstood their brief joys and dismissed their perpetual pessimism she could not be blamed. If she chose at this moment to change her life, completely, to make this her beginning, to say when I turn seventeen and go away I'll be free. I'll forgive everyone, she resolves, and who I can't forgive I won't remember. I'm cutting them off right here, that is the end of that life. I'm seventeen, I'm grown, no one controls me, I'll do everything new. Seventeen and the falling highrise she interprets as part of the magic and her newness and she wants to go back there and begin. She liked its confrontation, its concrete rudeness, its clarity.

There was a way that it stood against her plainly and right in her face. It did not deceive. It was against her from the beginning.

And her uncle, she had thought that he would join her in this, she had kept the light of his face, his head bowed against his beaten copper mask. She had had it in her head when she arrived that they would both be in the struggle. She had not known then that she would be leaving him, the bus eating the iron road hungrily under her; she did not know that she would leave him so easily, forgetting him before the bus was half a mile away.

"Don't go there and get into any foolishness you hear."

She doesn't know what to answer. She opens her mouth to say something or to smile but neither comes. There is a way when faced with her family she is speechless as a baby.

"This Black power thing, don't bother with them eh. Them all right."

She walks briskly towards the small building searching for the bus. She is a little ashamed at having to cry to leave. She cannot turn to him now and assert some adult point, she cannot tell him that she thinks that he is a failure. She can only wait for the bus pretending for this last moment that she is an obedient child taking instructions. They stand for the rest of the wait with nothing to say. Her body is damp with discomfort. Her uncle stands very still, Auntie Idrisse a little behind him.

Her clippings are her new past. Bits of newspaper are her history, words her family. She intends to walk right into the Movement when she arrives. The truth is she intends to find joy, just plain joy. They said go make something better of yourself. Well, joy would make her better and obviously joy wasn't in anything she'd seen so far. Not in the family, not in what they told her, not in working fields, not in eating, not in what passed for affection, not in family, cousins, brothers, uncles, aunts. Nothing back there could be called joy. And maybe she had to find out what her self was or change into her self. She knows that she'll never see her uncle and Auntie Idrisse again even though they've agreed that she'll just spend a weekend in Toronto and return to start school. They all know that the scheme won't work and they are probably as relieved to see her go as she is to leave. She looks at them waving, then going back to their car as the bus pulls out. Two Black people broken to the wind in Sudbury. She wonders if they know how lonely they look, how doomed. And what they will talk about now that they have no apprentice to anticipate or mould and no adopted child. She wonders if they tell the truth when they are together alone. She wonders if they talk, if it is possible to make out the deception any more or if the truth drying out on their faces makes them unable to finish a sentence or a laugh. She thinks of saving them but she is not that person yet; she is just happy to leave them and frightened. And ashamed of herself for crying and for leaving. Anyway she's going to Toronto to join the Movement.

The Greyhound glides through some darkening town. She switches on the reading light and rummages through her knapsack for her box. When her hand touches it she shuts the light off. She likes the dark outside the window and the swiftness with which it rushes by.

She wants to live in Che's line. She's memorized it, memorized it, "At the risk of seeming ridiculous, let me say that the true revolutionary is guided by great feelings of love." There is a way that she lands in the middle of that line, falls as if in love herself. She wants to live in all the poetry and all the songs, all the revolutionary words shooting the bus double time down the highway leaving her uncle's life of capitulation and dying. She knows that the minute she hits the subway, "Power to the People!" will bloom from her lips.

She is going to sit in rooms and argue that the revolution is going to come in her lifetime. And late nights beginning this July she will struggle for a more "scientific" understanding of that place that she's come from. She needs to understand it more fully than as paralysis, as making do, as calcifying the soul. She needs to understand what is now only impulse or reflex in her. She needs to pull herself out of inaction, the sloth the body feels if we can't do anything about life. Already with the distance, the ability to breathe has returned to her and to see. Already the body feels blood in places it hasn't gone. She knocks her head against books until five in the morning learning this new language. "It is impossible to think of a genuine revolutionary lacking this quality.... Our vanguard revolutionaries must make an ideal of this love of the people, of the most sacred causes, and make it one and indivisible...one must have a big dose of humanity, a big dose of a sense of justice and truth in order not to fall into dogmatic extremes, into cold scholasticism, into an isolation from the masses. We must strive every day so that this love of living humanity is transformed into actual deeds...." This language without hopelessness and inattention, so different from the words she'd heard all her life till now. "Is only God knows", "Is so things is", "God has a way for us". All of these words wash away in her new vocabulary.

The Movement is not hard to find. Her hair takes months to go back. The rooms are packed with sisters and brothers like her, excited and eager, who have, like her, awakened themselves. Their skin is electrified Black, burning. It is as if they suddenly became aware of its power where they had only known its weakness. Some days the rooms do not empty as they linger on the words of Samora Machel, the life of Patrice Lumumba, the question of what is to be done. She's learning so quickly it is as if her memory merely needed to be recalled.

What she will recall to her last minute is the crowd of them. May twenty-fifth, nineteen seventy-three. The late morning had not decided what to do, hot or cold, so it was warm. The crowd gathering like a sea, the skein of it sinuating from the park at Christie and Bloor to Harbord and Bathurst. She marched in the middle of it, near the front trying to look serious but wanting to laugh for the joy bubbling in her chest, the crowd around her like sugar, sugar is what she recalled, shook down her back by her sister, sticky and grainy and wanting you to laugh, and the shock and strangeness of her skin shaking sugar. The crowd like sugar down her back, sisters and brothers to the left and right of her marching. So much goes through her when the chant pushes from her lips, she wants to cry and all of her feels like melting into it, sugar. "Power to the People!" The crowd and her voice sugaring. If it was time to die she would die in here, in the middle of a crowd chanting "Power to the People!" They all know why this chant propels them along the winding way more than any other, it fills their mouths with all they need. And when they raise their fists it gushes from the tight folds. They need to feel outside of some power that holds them down. They all knew the extra meaning of what they did each day from sun-up to sundown, the kitchens, the rubber factory; they know the extra word here and the pay cheque less a few dollars and the secret pinch like the pinch of too small shoes, they know the blow that is not physical, near the heart and winching half the face open. They invent sugar. She marches along with the crowd, without the pain in her chest.

The first room is a room in the basement of a bookstore. Here she learns some of what her sleeplessness means. She's followed a poster to the room. Every other lamppost stapled with it all along College Street. *Free Brother Jamal. Imprisoned for defending the people against the racist fascist police state. The time is now. Defend our rights to self-determination.* "Welcome sister," someone says at the door but she doesn't hear even though these are the words she has waited to hear. Her body is soaking in sweat and before she sits down or notices the speaker at the front of the room, fogged in cigarette smoke, she clears her throat and says, "What can I do?" The room is quiet and she stands waiting and the room bursts out with laughter and she's waiting because even the laughter does not break the stunned air surrounding her body and her need to know. What can I do? Some hand tugs at her and the air collapses. She finds the room grinning and her own voice plaintive in her ear. She sits down next to the hand on her arm and the now eyes with laughter in them, the now face of someone smiling, the now warmth of the hand, the now mouth she has an unusual need to kiss because she's just heard "Welcome sister, sit down," and she sits but she still wants to know. What can I do?

It's hard to listen even though she's come to listen, but there's inside and outside of her and the blood gushing in her head and gasping at her ears muffles the voice of the speaker, though she hears him, wants to hear him. Something in her so new and she can't figure it out yet. She just knows that this time she does not have to watch. They need her to do something and they say — she knows — that at the end she will be a new person.

He says, "Brothers and sisters, we have lived through hundreds of years of slavery and oppression and the time has come to end our suffering. Don't be mistaken — we are not fighting for white folks to like us, we are not fighting to sit beside them in restaurants and buses, we are not fighting for mere equality with white people — we are fighting for liberation and liberation is none of these things. Liberation, brothers and sisters. Let me break it down for you. Are you tired of getting up in the morning with that ache in your back like you're lifting a load but you don't know what that load is? Are you tired of walking out in the street every morning feeling as if your life, your Black life and your Black self are just worthless? Are you tired of trying to do the best you can, following all their rules just like they told you and getting nowhere? That's not you brothers and sisters, that's the brutal ongoing system on your back. This backward capitalist system wasn't made for the benefit of Black people, it was made to exploit us, wring the life blood out of us and eventually kill us. And on top of that they blame us and make us blame ourselves — blame your mother, blame your father, blame the whole damn race — for not getting over. Self-hate is what it has to offer Black people, self-hate and self-destruction. We don't need to live like that, do we brothers and sisters? That's not living, it's the living dead. The only way out is to work in the struggle, the lifelong struggle for Black people's liberation. Brother Jamal is sitting in a cell for that. For our liberation...."

So simple, the words coming out of his mouth. So simple, slipping into a crevice in her back and in her memory, the thing uncomfortable about self-hate, like it was she and nothing outside of her, that it was some sickness she was born into, this feeling small, small in her heart. The screel of that winch creaking from her heart, her chest not able to bellow air and only in this room the blood begins to spread in its way.

"...All of the institutions in this society have collaborated against Black people. We, brothers and sisters, have collaborated against ourselves. The moment that Brother Jamal stood up to the pigs trying to arrest him for just being Black on the street where they thought that he shouldn't be, he was refusing to collaborate. Repression is the state's answer to non-collaboration...." In this room when she may be finally fully awake sleep might take her; these words rubbing her head might sleep her into another life.

"Sister, you want to sign up for a committee?" The meeting is over and the hand face mouth beside her belongs to a woman and she says, "Sister, you want to sign up for a committee? We need to poster for the rally against the Klan. I'm Abena."

"Verlia."

"We'll find you a new name soon. Listen..."

Quick as a whip and in the same hurry as she. Yes, she'll poster the width of this city, any city, and if she knows nothing now this room is full of all she'll need and it won't be long.

The pavement under her feet. There's nothing like it. And her blue canvas satchel, the weight of her stapler and the posters. That's now but the first time it was with paste in a bucket with a paint brush and running along the Danforth laughing... then along Bloor near Christie dodging... the cops she didn't know you had to dodge or else they'll charge you with defacing public property. The first time. A night after the first room. The poster rallying against the Klan in Riverdale. She was so nervous, the city all asleep because you had to poster then, late, with no one to see and call the police, no traffic, no people passing. Then just three of them for the area around Christie and Bathurst. She could hear her own footsteps and even talking softly their voices flew up the streets so they didn't need to shout to each other. She liked the sound of this, their voices humid like damp sheets in the asphalt cave of the road. And searing the leaves of posters to the splintered wood of the lampposts. First brushing the glue on the wood, laying the poster on and gluing again over the top. One eye on the street for the cruiser and one on the post. It took art as the message hung in the air. *Rally against the Klan. Fascists Have No Right to Speak.*

At the rally she sees hate. She's felt hate before but never seen it. Seen it arid and stark like that. She's felt it for sure what with the small evil sting of raw pinches in her childhood, primeval jealousies about food and toys, the vicious bites and cuffs of teenage fights after school and bigger. Scorn wandering by big people's houses, they wanting you to pass quickly lest your shabbiness infects them or dirties their yard. And yes, the imperious look of your betters in post offices, stores, government offices, hospitals, places you waited and waited in until some whim hit those you were waiting on. And anyway she had read reams and reams of it in books and newspapers, just the way it fluttered sometimes in ink or the way it chowed down as if eating beef, raw and bloody. So she'd read it and she'd known it just in the texture of her skin crawling under these words and the way everyone she knows talks in any room that she lives in as if they can assume the worst about their life and hang with something like shame. So she's felt hate and feels as if she knows it but nothing prepares her for seeing it. Feeling it is living with a chronic pain put seeing it is having a life-threatening attack.

He's skinny. And she can see his adam's apple and he's

wearing a white T-shirt and he's screaming at them, "Go back to where you came from! Go back to the jungle, niggers!" Next to him there's a woman. She looks at the woman unable to bear the cracking of his mouth. She looks at the woman expecting embarrassment, expecting her to calm him down, pull him away before he does something stupid, before his hatred overflows and swallows all of them including himself. She expects to find reassurance in the woman's eyes or fright for what he is about to do and that is why she exchanges his cracked mouth for the woman's face counting on some old familiarity to set the world right but it is Vee who is frightened when she finds a matching hate, devout and dangerous. And this also when she cannot bear the woman's eyes either moving her gaze down to the black T-shirt and the letters KKK burned into her left breast. Butterfly-like, raised bluish green. She moves her gaze again and it is her gaze now moving her head as if she were a doll made to move, so doll-like her head swings, stunned and slapped, to the woman's face again.

She had not expected it engraved on her breast. She had not even expected it in a woman. A man's hate she might have been ready for but not a woman's and not branded to the body. A kind of failure washes her, makes her turn away, the chant still going in her mouth, "Ban the Klan", drying. If she accepts that she shares something, anything, with them, this earth, a human body, the sweetness of breathing, the need to eat, saliva summoning pleasure, if she accepts this, then failure is what it all ends up being. The woman's severe brown hair, the detail of mascaraed eyes which she took in and the terrible appliqué. Well, hate looks like it's sudden and splits. Late July and she feels cold already. She's never experienced cold like the cold coming and she feels cold already. K. The eleventh letter of the alphabet trippling hotly on a woman's breast. Well she feels cold. Both of them, the man, the woman, screeching, "Fucking niggers! Fucking Jews! Get the fuck out of here!" Summing up the numbered skin of Jewish survivors and calculating the Black fists man-acled in air, they conceded only, "Fucking niggers! Fucking Jews!" And these two and a few others had come without their hoods, in the common ordinariness of T-shirts, in the plain declaration of a tattooed breast.

The next day she clips their photograph from a news-paper, the man's mouth still askew in the corner of his hatred, the woman not needing a word except the initials over her heart. She clips this photograph and she keeps it. Not to say haunting but hard not to return to if she declared herself human. Worse, them too. It gets lost as the years of political work pile on it in her room, as it yellows and tears and she never works it out or recovers or under-stands because it would be like understanding evil.

At three in the morning her eyes are laser clear, devouring all of the words and the words devouring her. Everything exists in the same time. If oppression exists she reasons, then freedom exists, the moment you see oppression you also see freedom so no one is ignorant or innocent. The world is less happenstance than deliberate. How to act then. That's the next thing. And if you recognize injustice then the moment arrives when you must act or say I accept this. This moment when the struggle is not just the dashiki and the romance of the skin, not just the satisfaction of getting history right and dancing at the Paramount. This moment, looking at the clipping of Angela Davis in chains or Bobby Seale gagged and chained and realizing that they are so close, so close, not only in the distance of a clipping but in the grief of a room with other brothers and sisters feeling the rough iron as if it were applied to their own limbs, the gag dry on their own tongue. How to act then when just like that, when everybody is asleep and you're alone in your room reading, you feel cracked open and close to this. How to act, what to do it for. The days that grind you down like a hill from rain, the days before you discover it's not just rain, nothing so easy and disinterested and you're the same as the day you discovered it and the day before you discovered it. You're the same.

You're the same. Whether you carry pamphlets or perhaps a crude kitchen knife into a corner store, a scythe for cutting down some crop, a spanner in a bicycle factory, a mop and pail, a white baby needing burping. You're the same. Perhaps you carry a tight ball in your heart over a four-year-old daughter who already won't amount to much, a son who'll stand on a corner with a bitter look in his eyes, perhaps you do not need another generation and the weary sentiment of mother love to feel bitterness just for yourself, just for your own life. What if you had chosen propping sorrow at a window, or reading dreams or walking out into the sea? Maybe after all you just know the everyday wrong you navigate and that is sufficient. And these make the privilege she's cut herself of flight, of reading late into the night and somehow staying safe in the fashion of words hard to do. Sane. But this is the moment when the public speeches lose their glamour and she is faced with her empty hands and her full head because all of a sudden the words she really wants to say are dangerous.

It's hard to see what's going on around you everyday as the hurt you need to fix, she knows. It's disbelief that does it. Your own doing or that muthafucker in your family trying to bring everybody down or them people over the street with no morals and no ambition. Their own stupid doing. It's a free country, right. Who's stopping you? It's your own doing why you're still here in life. It's disbelief that does it. It must be you. All that distance she needed just to figure that one little thing. Jesus, Jesus why does it take her so long when she should be ahead of this? She didn't get there by herself. She knows that, she knows that. She heard the murmur of it since she was born. It's our fault, it's our fate, God don't give you what you can't handle. Oh no, she didn't get there by herself. But if it took you by surprise, then surprise, and something like sickness at heart, standing on a street corner giving out leaflets for a rally against poverty. Surprise, one day when she held the paper in her outstretched hand for someone who passed saying, "I don't have time for this." It wasn't that she hadn't heard it many times before, it wasn't that she didn't have an answer for it. It was the sound of it, the I don't have a chance sound, the if you think some little piece of paper's gonna help me sound, the you must be crazy sound, the you're wasting your time if you think we're worth anything sound that made her stare.

She's listening and she has no patience for the line of fighting from within. She has no patience for the speaker who wheedles, "We don't hate white people."

"Who are you talking to brother, who are you reassuring? And tell me brother," she challenges, "what reasons do we have to love white people, enlighten us brother — why don't we hate them?"

She who knew waiting, she has no patience for patience. For going slow, for trumpeting the first Black to do this and the first Black to do that. Sellouts, grasping the few crumbs that fall from the table. She has no patience for bullshit about Black people needing an economic base. "We used to be white people's business, sisters and brothers. Do we want to join the man, brother, or do we want to do away with all of the mechanisms and trappings of the man?"

She will become part of a cell, the Committee for Revolutionary Struggle, that will send money, arms and revolutionary greetings to the MPLA in Angola, Frelimo in Mozambique, the PAC in Azania, ZAPU in Zimbabwe, the Panthers in Oakland. She talks to Akwatu X on the phone. "Brother, we would like you to come to Toronto and tell us about the situation in the States today. We know that the white liberals in the capitalist press have been gagged and news of our people's struggles is being suppressed so as to prepare the conditions for more repression." She will hear of discussions with the Black Liberation Army in upstate New York, "Urban warfare is the next step in the revolutionary struggle in America today," their manifesto reads. "The capitalist pigs have no intention of acting in the true interest of the oppressed Black people in this country. Their aim is to enslave us all and eliminate any opposition to their repressive state machinery. But no amount of payoffs, no amount of sellouts can change the will of the people to be free or blind people to the brutal nature of capitalist exploitation. We feel that at this time, living in the belly of the beast as we do, we must engage in armed clandestine strategies attacking the very heart of capitalism. We denounce the bourgeois strategies of accommodation as an abject and deliberate betrayal of the masses of Black people." She attends meetings of the Black Socialist Workers Party in Buffalo, visits the Ford Revolutionary Union Movement.

Sane. Saner than waiting for the world to happen to you.

There are two worlds here in this city where she arrives years earlier with a shoe box of clippings. One so opaque that she ignores it as much as she can — this one is white and runs things; it is as glassy as its downtown buildings and as secretive; its conversations are not understandable, its motions something to keep an eye on, something to look for threat in. The other world growing steadily at its borders is the one she knows and lives in. If you live here you can never say that you know the other world, the white world, with certainty. It is always changing on you though it stays the same, immovable, so when she helps children to read without an accent she teaches them by reading pamphlets on what to do when arrested. This warp is what the new world grows on. The new world growing steadily on the edge of the other. Her streets of barber shops and hairdressers and record stores and West Indian food shops bend and chafe to this swing. They pop up and shut down against this wind. A basement is a bar room and a dance hall, a bookshop and a place for buying barrels. A house sleeps twenty unrelated people except by colour and therefore destiny. A room upstairs a store is an obeah house, a place for buying oils, powders and thick warm Black hands massaging heads wrapped in white cloth to keep away evil. People bring all that is useful to a new place she discovers, not only their bodies to wrap around a drawer, a desk, a machine, a broom handle but they bring whatever spirits will help them out. And later she learns that she is not enough for this place and they are right not to have cut themselves as sparse as she; that late at night they have chants and acts which suffice because they cannot be explained. But that is later. She knows that you can live in a city which is divided even though there are no gates, no observable blockades. She lives in this city for years without talking personably to a single white person or having one talk to her. And that's a saving. Enough that they pull all your energy to fight them. She cannot imagine being friends with the enemy or that any one of them could surface from their city long enough to notice another human being. She is too busy learning other languages. She can live in this city and make it seem as if she's never left home. Except that everyone is from someplace else and the cadences are not the same, new rhythms have to be made and her mouth is like soft wire around these new sounds. She willingly changes, learning the brusqueness of Jamaican shopkeepers, the utilitarian logic of Nigerians, to mimic the sound of 'likkle', the way 'little' crackles on the

shopkeepers' tongues, to believe how earnest someone named
Ojo is. Except that everyone is from someplace else but this
city does not give them a chance to say this; it pushes their
confusion underground, it wraps them in the same skin and
slides them to the side like so much meat wrapped in brown
paper. So much meat they lapse into nostalgia about the
places before this one. She hates nostalgia, she hates this
humid lifeless light that falls on the past, it's too close for
her no matter how many years she spends away. Give her
these streets right now, hard as hell. She'd rather this any day.
When she first came face to face with that concrete highrise,
when she fell in love with its distance and grit she was not
mistaken. No ties, nothing hanging around your feet. She
hated what she already knew. Her people, gathered in barber
shops and tailor shops and basement parties reminiscing,
make her weak. She smells their seduction, it's the kind of
seduction that soothes the body going home on the train,
insulates it from the place of now and what to do about. It's
seduction that keeps them here for thirty years saying they're
going home some day, seduction that makes them take the
bit in their mouths, expect to be treated like dirt, brush past
her hand outstretched, a leaflet for a meeting fluttering.
Seduction, the sweet blurry feel of sun kissing their necks
that says that this will not last, this doesn't have to stay,
somewhere else we are other people. The hip-shotted walk
of the men, one leg heavy and lingering on possibility, one

leg light and ready for flight; and the women braced and girdled to hold in their regular sway, to saving the sweetness
collecting in their hips for some other time, some other
street, hoping it doesn't dry away. And working their heads
on how to squeeze that other job into the day, saving so that
they can live some other place. All this thinking of another
place. Well she was there and doesn't want to go back. Give
her the day-to-day hardness, real and here. She didn't want
to be anywhere but now, nowhere but the what to do about.

That is why she'd joined the cell not wanting to limp
home in the embrace of where she used to be. So give her
the coldness of the afternoon she got arrested for kicking a
cop, yelling pig into his face and having him bend her arm
back until she felt her shoulder leave its lock. A weekend in
jail waiting for them to let her go and keeping quiet under
their "Black bitch! Black whore! Nobody's coming to get
you out." They didn't know but she'd kept herself quiet
repeating Che's words to herself. "At the risk of seeming
ridiculous... at the risk of seeming ridiculous... let me say
that the true... let me say that the true... true revolutionary
is guided... the true revolutionary is guided by great feelings
of love..." Over and over again taking the sentence from the
middle or wherever her thoughts happened on it, "... guided
... true... of seeming ridiculous... great feelings... at the
risk... of love." She had jumbled that sentence every way
and always its centre was light and soft, nothing abandoning

in it, nothing asked for. She had closed her eyes dreaming into its core and who it would take to be those words, who she would have to be. That is how she staved off the dread creeping in on her and the panic collecting like a surprise in her throat. When she wanted to scream because she could not stand being confined, when she had to calm herself, when only three days in jail felt like a lifetime, she twisted those words and dreamed them around again and again. So on Monday, when she was finally released into the worried and angry faces of her comrades, she stepped towards the cop who had undone her shoulder. She wanted to say something like Che, something tippling off the tongue full of all her anger but peaceful in the end, reconciled to his instinct. *You are nothing but an instrument of the ruling class, a brutish automaton lacking humanity, used to repress the body and spirit of the people.* Something like that. She wanted to say something to read him back to his mother's womb; something to wrench his own flesh from its bone as he'd done hers. When it came out of her mouth it wasn't only out of her mouth but first her finger marking his face, an old gesture marking an enemy, and then she spat on the floor in front of him. "Never have a day's peace. Look for me everywhere." Such an old curse creeping out of her. She did not remember learning the gesture. And this too then Che, wrath. Look how it raised her hand in an old sign, look how it sprang water from her mouth. That day her reputation for coolness began though some in the cell said that she was undisciplined and lectured her about "unnecessary confrontation" bringing too much attention to the cell and "jeopardizing future actions." But give her the clamminess of an early morning a year later, cigarette- and whisky-filled, her hands trembling on the steering wheel waiting for Akwatu to break the window with fire no Aryan literature could survive, no Aryan pulse perhaps either. It took her weeks to stop shaking even after the news had died down, even after they'd disappeared until the news died down, even after that. But give her that feeling of being followed around, hair sweating under her arms and waking up in the middle of sleep drenched in fright. For six months after she just went to work and came home not talking to anyone in the cell, watching television and going to the movies. Even visiting a still wary but pleased aunt. The aunt thinking that she'd come around perhaps because she didn't talk about the struggle, the struggle, the struggle and who said what, and read this, and how they were all just sellouts.

Abena had not joined the cell with her. She'd said that she didn't feel that the struggle was at the armed stage yet and that Verlia had better be careful about what she was getting into.

"You can't be ahead of the people," she'd said. "The people have to be with you."

"It's never going to be the time. Is it the people or you?" Spinning that laser-sharp eye on Abena. She'd noticed her measured opinions in all the meetings, making sure and warning to be careful, down to whether this or that action was necessary and what night to poster and how to speak. At first she'd listened, taken it as wise and then she'd begun to itch under all that warning, to feel as if she were being dosed with fear.

"When is it going to be the time?" She could feel Abena measuring her breath and she felt ungrateful and as if she were betraying her. But when? Every communion has some betrayal anyway — every time you touch someone, every time you open your mouth — so she had a right to ask when. Maybe Abena was hiding something, maybe there was some reason that wasn't really about the struggle at all but personal.

"Do what you want."

"No, I really want to know," guilty but somehow wickedly. "When the hell is the time? You have to leap sometimes don't you? Sometimes you have to be ahead? We all don't get it at the same time, do we?"

"Fine, you have all the right answers. Do what you like."

"But answer me if there is an answer. Stop acting this way because we fuck for Christ' sake. What are the conditions? When will the time be right?"

"Because we fuck? Who taught you anything? Including fucking!"

They were cooking, something warm after a vigil for South Africa. That glass-towered Canada Place where their chants bounced back and forth against the stalactites of business and money. Hoping that they heard them on the twenty-fourth floor. Hard to lay siege to a glass tower. Hoping to be an inconvenience at least. Hoping to freeze the air exhaled into the cold Friday evening and freezing instead their feet, their hands, their own breath. But hoping to make fire. Left when everybody else had gone home not persuaded by "Come, we'll cook," but wanting to get to their own beds out of the cold. Left to the two of them still wide awake and their hands with nothing to do. Cooking after and freezing in their own knowledge on the floor of her room. If desire could freeze and burst on the floor. Flood the room with her crying. Sometime in the night she sits up and holds herself. What they've done, how she couldn't stop crying and how she couldn't explain bawling like that, how some sweet and awful thing had happened. She couldn't explain it to herself crying like that, wracked with it, her legs not staying still, falling loose at the circle of Abena's neck. If desire could break you just so by surprise and not harm you. Sometime she feels Abena fold her wholly and they are stooping, doubled and kneaded in sweat and where she begins and Abena ends the skin does not break off, yet it does, but rides in oil and rolls. The floor is wet with their sweat and oil and the slick of limbs and their shake and sudden, sudden sweet hastes. Her own mouth suddenly too, soft and greedy, in its own suck and circles. So much water.

The room is full of water. Her hands are salt. Her hands are slippery. And the room is so full of water she is frightened. Sleep is not different but part of their mouths on thick flesh, blades, in the shoulder, the thigh, the arms finally bracing the walls unable to keep themselves inside their own muscle. She falls asleep in the melt of room and water and oil and Abena, someone else herself by then. Someone waking up not knowing what to say, sprawled in Abena's body and unable to peel herself off. And Abena, feeling her tense and balk, murmured in her own sweet sleep, "Don't worry, don't worry. I won't . . ." Won't what? Won't say. Won't tell. Won't remember. Won't hold you to it. Won't die. Won't hate you. Won't want you. Won't come back. Too many possibilities wake her fully. If she thought that it would go away or be the same or easily denied or not matter after, this sleeping assurance of secrecy makes her sad and hungry for declaration. Lying there asleep Abena expects nothing of her, she's already calculated that all that could be hoped for is something silent. What loneliness. She waits for Abena to wake up to tell her, "I'm here too you know," even if it is without conviction to start but, yes, here she was, naked and folded in her so she was here and no way her hand could avoid the well of Abena's back and no way her body did not like this and wasn't surprised.

"God Verlia. You're so much work. All right, the conditions for armed struggle. When the people have had enough and by their manifestations acknowledge that the regime has become so repressive as to force them to take up arms. Arms are not the first resort and should not be taken up in an act of dilettantism or overzealousness but in a genuine and serious attempt to seize power."

The cell had worked above ground for a while. Political education in the public housing buildings, down Regent Park and in the east end where there were fights between the West Indians and the Nova Scotians. Bitterness and hostility turned inside out. Two sets of Black people fighting each other over turf as if any turf could be theirs without the white man's say so. Not that it didn't work, pointing out who the real enemy was, but hell they knew that. No news to them, but they were closer to each other, the white man wasn't real and anyway couldn't be touched. They needed a real example of how, not any bunch of students telling them what they learned in books. Unless the cell could show how you could actually touch the man the West Indians and the Nova Scotians would just continue to bust each other's heads at the Paramount every Saturday night.

"So meanwhile what? Meanwhile take shit, demonstrate, sing 'We Shall Overcome' and be an open target? No fucking way. Your material conditions don't work here. We have to go underground, agitate and strike blows against the racists and the imperialists."

She'd followed Abena the first couple of years. She'd

leapt into her mouth and her eyes the first time she'd seen her and she'd fallen into her hurried movements. Make the flyer, mobilize the people against this injustice and that one, the schools, the police, the hospitals, the street lights, the housing project, this one in jail, that one beaten up, that one fired, this one spat on. But it had begun to seem endless, useless, and she hated that feeling. Just like home again. She needed to move, feel light. She didn't come all the way here to get beaten down again. And nothing, no assurances that the struggle would triumph like this, and be patient — none of that was enough. She didn't want to wake up tomorrow and tomorrow and tomorrow feeling the same, in the same spot. People tied you down, all their fear and weakness tied you down, all their desire blinded them. She wanted distance from that; she'd had enough of people falling over each other, blundering through, doing things by mistake or pleasure.

Well Abena hadn't joined and had forgiven her or at least left the argument alone whenever Vee appeared at her door sweating because she couldn't sleep for fear of being watched, followed. She was all adrenalin, so tense after every action that her eyelids jumped uncontrollably. Abena just let her in and stayed up with her. A factory, a cop, smuggling someone across the border, they didn't talk about it. They didn't make love either. Verlia became nervous. She would freeze when Abena made a sound and she would cry when they did make love, she would weep, say she felt too open when too open was what she used to want. They both noticed how she lost weight and smoked more and more and drank more and more.

"You're not going to be good for this soon."

"It's just my body. My head's straight."

"You need to work above ground for a while."

"Maybe," warily.

She was deep in thirteen winters when she observed the stringiness which had overtaken her mind. The cell has been her life here. Holding her together like family, it's the only family she can bear. Comradeship chosen, friendship that was not chance or biology. When the movements in Africa triumphed, such as they did, the cell turned to organizing for the people at home. And there was so much to be done for the community outgrowing simple familiarity. She no longer knew almost everyone any more and gradually all the greetings shared, the power to the people brother and sister faded into vague nods of anonymity. Some of the people in the cell left, went to Zimbabwe to join the Patriotic Front or to Guyana to join Walter Rodney. She stayed. She missed them, missed the noise, and the constant urgency and had the feeling that what was coming would not be as simple or clearly identifiable. Fighting the system here had driven them away or ground them down somehow. And little by little without her noticing after the comrades left for Zimbabwe and Guyana and after the cell lost so many people to tiredness and had worn itself away in argument and blame for small, small failures, she fell in again with Abena's airless busyness. One thing, she didn't know how Abena kept it up, just content with breaking rules, a passport here for someone running, a car to Buffalo, a health card, a pay cheque under the table. Small things, Abena said, small things are the only things you can do sometimes. It rankled and besides it wasn't true, but just because she was tired and sometimes so frightened, she'd fallen into it, and because she was losing her comrades and needing someone to reassure her that there was a way, and really there were people needing a car to Buffalo and a health card and money under the table and a place to stay.

She was walking from work, leaning against a late November rain when she missed tamarinds, sour and stringy, and then she missed — bright bright, pooled and mountainous pink or yellow at the side of a road — branches of a poui tree hanging over. What had made her miss them was the last woman she'd seen today. She'd come into the office where she now worked with Abena seven days a week. Seven days a week because they both needed seven days to work themselves into the tiredness they needed to feel they'd done something. So the woman came in, she was freezing, hiding, well what did it matter, hiding. From a man, from the police, from people, from God. At first Vee had been brisk and enthusiastic with her, the same briskness and enthusiasm as

Abena to say to her people that all is possible, you just have to know the system and you can figure it out. It was a game or rather a skill. No, no no, seriously, listen, these people make rules to exclude us, she would say, so it is not necessary to follow them, you're working against yourself if you do. That's how it was now. It had started out more straightforward, finding the revolution, bringing down the system, organizing into cells, study groups, action groups, demonstrating, waiting. Now, shit, breaking these fucking rules was the revolutionary act. Fine, fine fine fine. The woman sitting in front of her didn't need pessimism. Straighten up Vee, straighten up, she told herself. If there could be just one moment when she would be without the weight in her head of airlessness, of not belonging, that would be the moment. Now she was waiting. Now she was waiting for all of it to end in the place she wanted to live and she depended on that moment coming, that's all she was hanging on for now and she told these women coming to her office day after day that it was coming and it lead her body in all its motions. The most mundane and hopeless ones. The times when the hall had to be opened and the food ready and the speaker brought and when the phone calls had to be made and the children comforted and the excursion buses booked.

And now this woman had come in running from God, just before a November rain and after thirteen Novembers she was ready to tell her how to do it, brisk and enthusiastic as ever and the weight of the woman sitting before her heavier than the weight of her belly and the woman's face crumbling like porous stone and Vee couldn't summon it up even one last time. So she remembered tamarinds, sour, seedy and stringy but eaten voluntarily. And without reason she started to cry and the woman cried too. They could not dig themselves out, buried underneath the pods, brittle and sandy, their fingers sinking into the cracked fruit and the taste in their mouths springing water and bringing more tears to their eyes. The tiny mimosaed leaves, the spindly branches, that you cannot hold or hang on to, hanging from their faces. They leaned against the rough bark and belly of the tree, the feel of it ripped their ears bloody and they could not stop crying, trying to find their way back to the room where they were sitting. Pods of tamarind, fingery, fingery, falling into the room. She opened her mouth and nothing like assurance could come out, just the piquant taste of tamarinds and the taste of tears, saline, tepid and tasteless, the way tears are indifferent. It was the taste of tears that stopped her, the liquid indifference from her own eyes. Her face heated and swollen, her eyes so full they closed, yet the cool taste of tears. Why her tears did not taste brackish as they should, how hopeless can the body be, how on its own, how determined to be. Here this cool taste washing her tongue, tepid and dry. It led her, this coolness, as if she shared her body with someone else more sanguine, as if she were imposing, presumptuous even, it led her out of the room, making a bed for the woman in the back saying, "Don't worry. Tomorrow we'll figure it out." Laughing, saying, "But look at me. You come for help and I'm crying with you." Making the woman laugh too.

November is not a good time to be sad or worried or in trouble, she knows. Three-quarters of the sky is always grey and closed in on the city. The sky swaths your head like the bandages of an injury to the brain. It isn't a time to make decisions, it isn't a time to look too closely at your life, or the street you live on or your own face for that matter, leave that for June or July she knows. It's waiting time. Time when she plans nothing but waiting. This is what a sky like a bandage over a wound does to her. Makes her wait, makes her hold everything. It's the one thing she cannot help, the effect of the sky on her disposition. The city is a construct of shells, glass and aluminium, brick and concrete, it hardens like a beetle, scarabaeus and shiny-eyed, just to avoid a November and what comes after. But all of this thickening and shelling can only do so much and the eyes unlucky enough to be without scales must look to the real sky sometime. Then November is a tragedy of scarred trees and rumpled clothes, of the skin's defensive shrivelling, of huddled shabby bus-stops and a wind ready to ice and crumble the bone. The city shrivels, its plastic skin roughens scabrous, and people bow their heads to the tunnels underneath and to impatience till April or May. Rain then is luck in November. If it is warm enough to rain then it's luck. Though rain here is no display, just inconvenient; it has no dirt to fatten and muddy, no great winds to make it fearful, no ground to seep into but the orderly sewers. She will take rain if not snow, rain, soundless and windless. Cocoons of concrete sheath the life of this city, above and below anticipating what comes after. It's no betrayal to say that it overwhelms you as much as it clothes you. No betrayal at all. She can't help thinking that there's a shadow across her eyes, that the year is ending, but more, her life is ending. She can't help thinking that she is shedding and dying. She cannot get into step. But betrayal occurs to her. Is she running out on herself? It occurs to her and that early morning walk from the bus station that first morning when she said, "This is where I'll live. This is where I'll make my life. This is who I'll forget. This is what I'll remember."

The tumbling tumbling of missing, undoing for no reason except the used to, the first seen, not even the understood. Most of life is so much pattern, so regular, so slight. The routine of poui, dry season or rainy is all she misses. Misses. Missing is unravelling though. Will she become one of those women standing at Bathurst and Bloor, looking into the window of some store, plastic bags in her hand, looking into the window but not looking, forgetting that she is looking into the window because she is seeing some other place, as if she is looking up a rain forest mountain road thinking, "When I will get a transport?" One of those, her face slipping into the shape of a wall until she forgets coming home to take it off, one of those giving up her children to a city beyond her control, or to water between them and an airplane, saying, "I do my best. I send for them." This woman standing at the store window, she . . . you do your best if you don't know yet that it's best you do nothing. Doesn't matter what you do. Turn her . . . your back, it's the better choice. Leave. Will she become one of those women arrested in the long gaze of better memories even if they weren't better, just not here? Not here. Here. There is no way of marking, no latitude or longitude, a black sand seabed, a lagoon of alligators, no discernible inclines or shapes, here is a sea belly deep and wide, to float or drown so many bodies, here is leaving, here is a highway and a house inhabited by strangers but it's called home and the wood, you do not know who nailed the wood, who tarred the ground, here your hands look unfamiliar, you say, "Are these mine? I don't recognize them." Here is a hole in a wall opening to the sea and you . . . she cannot recognize anything after that . . . she cannot remember why you . . . she is standing at a corner called Bathurst and Bloor looking into a store window, looking back from the sea, "I'd better run across the street, take the bus to Vaughan. But if only this were here, the sea . . .

well..." Here is not a word with meaning when it can spring legs, vault time, take you ... her away in a store window and a palmed mountain road, a tunnel in a wall leading to the sea, here she memorized the road and here she forgot, she recognizes nothing not even her hands, here she ... you can vanish into the bus, her plastic bags, the traffic going by takes bits of your hair, and things you have thought, here is nothing to hold on to or leave a mark, here you ... hold on to your name until it becomes too heavy and you forget it. She thought, until here, missing is not simply in your life, it strikes you at the store window, at the wall to the sea and what comes after, here does not hold still, you absorb it and it ... you disappear.

So in the November rain Vee is thinking of tamarinds. Tamarinds that cut the roof of her mouth. Tamarinds she never really liked, not as much as Pomeracs, perfumed, velvet and red. Then of pools of purple dust on the side of the road under a lilac tree hanging. Then pink mountains, tumbling mountains of poui petals. Then of stray dogs mangy and lurking in rubbish heaps, then of a hill dry and burnt, then of red hibiscus going wet and limp under her thumb and forefinger, then of juice running down her elbow, the leering yellow face of mango in both her hands, then of sugar cutting her tongue, then of an ochre daub of earth jutting up, then of braying far off, then of water sucking into a conch-laden rock, then of shell pink from sea wash. Worst of all November is when she misses hot hot lascivious colour.

November is when missing plumes, it plummets. Though for the life of her, why poui and immortelle? Why not someone, Tante Emilia and her reading of dreams? Why not those mornings, Tante Emilia staring her in the face to wake up and tell the dream? Why not she, rubbing redemption oil on her head so that she could fall asleep and dream the big dream? Why not longing for what has happened to her family, for who must surely have died already, who is still waiting with the same sighs, the same sucking teeth, the same hands brushing resignation? If not longing for voices she will recognize without hearing, why colour? She only ever wanted to miss what was essential. She wanted to miss nothing there. But it is simple, she misses colour and nothing else. Simply. It is not food or rain or clothing or fresh water or whisky but she misses it like drink, as if she's thirsty. Especially this November, especially today, especially... especially when the woman sleeping in the back office, running from God knows who, made her hunger for it and tamarinds.

She might on a day like today decide to go back. Go back for something so small. Or she might walk all the way up Bathurst in the drizzle thinking of tamarinds and where things were now. But it would have to be something small in the end.

Had anyone told her she would not have believed that she would wake up in this room. This morning is shedded in light and dust. That wooden window will open. The hand opening the wooden window will be the hand of the woman I sleep with in this room. I have never been in such a room. A wooden room. The updraft of air through the floor boards is strafed in slivers of salt and smoke. It is a room where I will open my eyes and the woman opening the window will be the woman I will live with for ever. I will not look at her, I know her face, it is melting into the soft sun she lets in with her hand on the window. I do not need to look at her face, it is the face melting into the sun at the window. This morning the chacalaca birds warn of rain coming, my eyes do not need to open to see her eyes look for rain through the window where her face is melting. I told her I could dance the mash potatoes.

She liked the weight of her, solid and permanent against her. She liked her wayward legs; in sleep they straddled her hips and when they lay plush on their own side of the bed Verlia awoke feeling lonely, pulling the woman towards her, comforted in the thighs lapping against her. It was usually close to morning when she missed her, when she reached over and felt for her, hoping that she was there and sensing another thing, the room full of hoping. She knew that she was safe with a woman who knew how to look for rain, what to listen for in birds in the morning, a woman who loved to feel her face melting in the sun in the morning through a window. She needed a woman so earthbound that she would rename every plant she came upon. She needed someone who believed that the world could be made over as simply as that, as simply as deciding to do it, but more, not just know-ing that it had to be done but needing it to be done and sim-ply doing it. This is what she wanted to believe and what she always had doubts about, and when they'd first met she thought that she was the one who knew everything, and how she was going to change this country woman into a revolu-tionary like her, but then something made her notice that she was the one who had doubts and what she was saying she merely said but Elizete felt and knew. When Vee's bright-ness wore down by four in the afternoon, when wielding a machete blistered her hands and she tried to still keep going and when she did the wrong thing by working through the midday sun and when her eyes looked longingly at them liv-ing their life and not looking at it like she, she had to laugh at her damaged soul. That she would envy hardship, that she would envy the arc of a cutlass in a woman's hand. That she would fall in love with the arc of a woman's arm, long and one with a cutlass, slicing a cane stalk and not stopping but arcing and slicing again, splitting the armour of cane, the sweet juice rushing to the wound of the stem. That the woman would look up and catch her looking and she would hate herself for interrupting such avenging grace.

What made her notice that she was the one needing was that grace, that gesture taking up all the sky, slicing through blue and white and then the green stalk and the black earth. Anyone who did that all day, passed through everything that made up the world, whose body anchored it, arc after arc after arc, who was tied to the compulsion of its swing, who became the whirl of it, blue, white air, green stroke, black dust, black metal, black flesh, anyone with such a memory would know more, be more than she. Looking up from her exercise in duty and revolutionary comradeship, looking up from the task that she did not have to do but only did in order to come close to the people, she would watch a whole field, mile after mile of whirling, each person caught up in their own arc of metal and dust and flesh until they were a blur, whirring, seeming to change the air around them. Then this world went away from her.

She had left herself so bare this woman could see her braised skin. This woman she was ready for.

She'd never thought of men like that. Her breasts in the curve of a woman's is how she'd imagined it. Some of the women with whom she'd sat late in her room in Toronto drinking beer, she'd thought of in the crook of her arm, in the curve of her back, in the slope between her legs. But to appear normal she had slept with men at first. Slept with was hardly the phrase, certainly not fucked. Sex. Yes, she had sex with men until one day she couldn't have it any more, just couldn't and returned to the thought of her breasts in the curve of a woman's, her legs wide to her tongue, her lips warm to her face, the fat of her belly, her hands searching her back, easing her muscles, watering her thighs. She's thought of the brush and ease of the skin, the melt into the soft and swell of the body. How this is sometimes not done, not spoken, in her room, the beer at their lips, the moment with nothing to say between them. Then sometimes she would fall asleep in the curve of breasts, in the crook and keen musk of thighs, the slip of the skin.

She wants nothing more. Not the bed that comes with it, not the kitchen, not the key to the door. She hates the sticky domesticity lurking behind them. She doesn't want wanting more. Just her sparse room, sparse, sparse and clear, just the empty floor and sometimes a woman with her back to kiss, her company to keep all night.

The first day here. I have trouble recalling why I came. When you come to a totally new place to which you've made a political commitment and when you arrive you're not sure if it is the right place because it never is the place you conjure up in your head.... I've made this trip so many times and yet this time I am so tired. I have to keep reminding myself to stand straight. If I've made a mistake I will find out but this feeling is just tiredness. The Caribbean always devastates me. Just the landscape and my childhood seem to take me over once I'm here. But I suppose one month will go by and then another. By St. Vincent, all of my resolve was gone. I lost my traveller's cheques three times, once in the hold of the LIAT, twice just in my wallet. Just the warm close air when the airplane door opened frightened me. I smelled everything I was in that air, all my doubts. I

hate that smell, it sits me in my childhood like
a useless baby. Everything made me feel like
turning back.

Saw a flat today, but it's too dark. Jesus, it
reminded me of a basement apartment in Toronto.
I'm going to look for something brighter. They
showed me a place on a hill but there's no trans-
portation up, just foot. I'll have to walk everyday
but maybe it will be good for me. If you're in the
struggle you're in the struggle Verlia.

I must remember that people are different
here. I must listen first, watch carefully. Perhaps
I am not honest enough. I don't express my fears
right away. I discover them. I have to admit
them. It's really some colonial shit happening
with me. All this fear for a place I should know.
I feel very nervous here. I never got to know this
place because I spent so much time running
from my family. Anyway I hope that I can see
my way somehow. I probably won't even have
time to think about it. We're starting right away
with the cane workers. Well, everyday I must
drag myself up, caution myself. It's easy to lose
faith quickly. I'm reading about Cayetano

Carpio. He says that through "the necessity of immolating oneself in the crucible of practice, one could affirm it as a test, and see if we were capable of translating theory into practice. And this only life itself could tell us." Well, I'm there Cayetano. The crucible of practice.

I can't pick up the short wave. Feeling far away from Abena and everyone at home. Over here I feel far away from the world. Especially at night. Anyway I'll see her in July. Slept late today, then went into town which is not far. Walked. Bought postcards to send back to Toronto. Went to the post office for stamps. Then discovered the public library. Dismal. Colonialism is a bitch. Went to lunch at an obviously tourist dive. It looks as if a German fellow owns it. You wonder how they get all the way here. Then walked back to the office. I have not been utterly faithful to this diary. I'm writing this on the twelfth. At first I though I'd do it at the end of each day but only gloomy thoughts come to me then. So it is not convenient to do that or wise. There was a party in the house tonight. They were talking about the night of the revolution, about how Desmond

Jackson took a boat to Trinidad and that the prime minister there was enraged and wanted him off the island. He had to get back on the same boat and come back. Jackie Williams was there too. Desmond made a sexist joke and Jackie said maybe I should leave the room. She must have thought that I was very young. She gave a good joke about Reagan and Brezhnev and Manley in a car together. Afterwards I went to bed.

Slept quite late. I was supposed to go to a youth rally but didn't. Stayed home trying to get used to being here. In the night I listened to the BBC and in the day I slept and looked out at the harbour. The nights are not so great, but then again they've always been a problem anywhere for me. I don't know why. I called Abena and became sad. I don't know why. She sounded sad. My imagination or my period.

Went into town, bought letter forms, stamps, envelopes, had lunch at some preten-tious place run by an American. That will pass. I must have gone in there unconsciously. Met

with my supervisor about the job. Reading
CLR's *Dialectic and History.*

It's been three months since I've bothered
with this account. I cannot write this diary in
the night. The nights here always fuck me up.
I don't look forward to them. Tonight though
was a good one. I sat outside till quite late
drinking tea. I got Radio Moscow for about
five minutes. I'm looking forward to the days
when I'll be working so hard that I'll be too
tired to think about the nights. I took the
house on the hill. At least I can see things
coming. It was painted an awful pink so I had
to redo it. They're sending me to Caicou to
work with the cane workers. They haven't
expropriated all the land for fear of external
repercussions and there's a son of a bitch up
there who is robbing the workers blind and
they're too scared to touch him. We have one
collective there willing to move on him but
they need an organizer.

I'm getting into the rhythm. I made my first
trip up there last week just to see what it was
like. Going up on the bus I saw men and

women working the roads. The bus stopped
for a boy bringing food to his mother on the
road crew. Near a river there were stones and
women washing and then the heat made the
bus break down. We waited. I have to learn
patience and this is a good place to do it. We
waited until the radiator cooled again, fanning
ourselves in the still, still heat. Then Caicou.
If cane fields can feel oppressive they do here
and there was a silence. I only saw one or two
people at first. It was the middle of the day
and I had arrived at the wrong time. Most
work gets done in the mornings when the
sun is not so hot. When I arrived people had
gone home or stopped for lunch. Why I have
forgotten all of this is beyond me but the
fields are enough for me to remember. That
waving stillness made everything come up
in my throat.

I saw this woman there. I tried to say something to her but she passed by as if I had said
nothing. It will of course be very difficult to
convince people, but she told me plainly and
without saying so that they don't trust me. I
am thirty years and one month old today.

All the names of places here are as old as
slavery. I've learned some in the weeks going to
Caicou along Eastern Road. The transport
passes Choiselles and Morne Diablo and
Arima and La Chapelle. These small places,
somewhere like where I come from. Morne
Rouge and Fer de Lance and Moruga and
Dead Man Bay, Las Cuevas and Petit Homme
and Gros Homme. The meanings underneath
are meanings I don't know even though I was
born somewhere here, but I can hear in the way
people say them, the driver on the transport
calling them out "Choiselle! Talk fast, talk
fast!" and the old women passengers, "Morne
Diablo, darling, let me down there." "Saint
Michel sweet boy, take a dollar." "You in a
hurry or what? Look drop me by Petit Homme
eh!" I've never said the name of a place like
this, dropping darling and sweet boy and eh
after them. You would have to know a place for
that and I don't really know anywhere. But I
enjoy the way they say it. I could ride this bus
all day listening.

Went every day to the field the last while.
She's watching me. The woman who won't talk

to me. I can feel her in the field as if she's looking at me, but when I look over all I can see is her swing. I can feel her like a body against me and she's hundreds of feet away. I know that I can't keep up with them but I'm trying to pull my weight in the field. I don't know if this will help but I think it's important to show the people that I am not just a mouthpiece — that I can work hard too. This may not work of course because I have to put myself in their place. I at least can leave and they know that but I think that if I show that I am in the struggle with them…

The list of workers is coming along. The old ones whom the owner wants off "his" land make me weep. Sin is not a word I use but I've seen what it might look like. They are so old their eyes are ink blue, navy and watery. They must have been here since slavery. They make me think that's truly possible.

I've been reading Che again. I get so much there. He says the revolutionary "is consumed by uninterrupted activity that comes to an end only with death unless the construction of

socialism is accomplished on a world scale."
He tells me how much harder I have to work.
I feel so small sometimes. I know that that is
just my family crawling through, saying be satisfied with being alive, and it weakens me to
think of them. I don't want to go back to that.
This place that Che talks about, when this
weakness is transformed into people living as
they can, cleanly. I suppose I must have believed
my family. They can always reach me in that
small place in me no matter how many years I
put between us. And this place so reminds me
of them.

I don't allow myself to have arguments with
the other comrades but I think that this will
be a slow, slow process. You can't rush people,
and five-hundred years is a long time to undo.
Some of the comrades are, I feel, a little
overzealous, talking to older people as if they
are their betters. Sometimes I suppose I do
it too and I have to watch myself. How can
I look an old man in his blue-black eyes and
tell him what he needs to do? There is so much
fear and a landlord in a Jeep Cherokee with
a gun...

Now I fall asleep like a dead weight every
night. I can't keep my eyes open past eight. It
matters that here the darkness is so deep your
eyes can't help but close. I am doing so much
work that I can sleep deeply most nights. But I
am tired, tired, tired.

I don't know why I started this. I suppose I
was lonely and it was a way of talking to
myself or talking to someone. "Only life itself
could tell us." I wonder if Carpio felt the mix
of lethargy and rage that I feel. This place
holds you down with an unweighable load. I
feel as if I'm in that sleep that you want to
wake up from but cannot and then you dream
that you are awake only to find yourself asleep.

Sick today can't go to work.

Sick.

Jesus! My grandfather's diary had this in it
before he died. Sick today.

What I want to know, Che, is if you ever
wake up and it is all all right.

People get so abusive when they get drunk. I suppose whatever is in you comes out. In Toronto I used to avoid the buses and trains especially on nights after baseball games or football games. Race would just float those liquored lips like something suppressed so long it comes up vile. Here, the hatred is stiff, it chews itself and mumbles. I can never make out the words outside my window on Friday nights, I just know that they mean no good. . . . I wonder if I don't want to understand them. They sound so hateful with women screaming at the end of them.

It's not only my family. It's the fact. Fact. Fact. Intangible fact of this place. It's not possible to get rid of that. So much would have to have not happened. It's like a life sentence. Call it what we want — colonialism, imperialism — it's a fucking life sentence. Nobody I come from knows these words but they do the time. You can't catch five fucking minutes of sleep without it, you can't drink a beer, some fucking breeze passes over your lips smelling of molasses, you can't even fuck, some pain shows up and you weep like a fucking ocean.

I think that I'm getting used to living here again. I'm past the major crisis. Yet I can't help thinking that it was a bad time to leave. I miss my friends there. They were my family. Who am I kidding, I was in deep trouble there. I had to go on a long walk up Bathurst and down Wychwood talking to myself because I had fallen into a kind of numbness of mind, a wastefulness. So in a sense this trip has rescued me. I felt wounded all the time and I was so anxious I couldn't sleep. Enough. But I am growing.

I have to wake up early in the mornings to go the market to get the transport to Caicou. There's a sepia light then and the market women come down on the transport that I take up. Sleep is in all our eyes and there's the smell of spice and seasoning on them.

I am now living on Archibald Street. I'm such a light sleeper that every dog that runs under my window wakes me up. Also, there's a breadfruit tree in the yard that rains aborted breadfruit all night, scaring the hell out of me. My neighbours here are not as colourful as the ones in French Town who were poor people,

prostitutes and destitutes. There was a whore
house, if you can call it that, two doors above
me and a place called Miss Jean's Bar where
they played Joni Mitchell loudly. I struck up a
conversation there once with a man who asked
me if I wanted any weed and told me about the
regional trade. He was from St. Vincent but
hiding out here for awhile, until time to go
north. Then he told me that he was going to
Canada to pick apples or grapes and that he
had already greased an official's hand to get on
the work gang. He was planning to skip the
farm and go to the States as soon as he could.
He said the migrant workers scheme was a real
rip-off because you didn't get the money they
said, but that if you bought or stole a lot of
clothes and electrical things you could bring
them back to sell.

Things are in a kind of lull now. There was
an alert in September. Threat of invasion. But
that is over. Also, the rainy season is upon us.
Yesterday we went to the beach and it was dead.
After a week of rain the sand at the bottom
of the sea had shifted and levelled out so that
you could go fairly far out without getting

deep. There's water everywhere and it is quite
humid.

I just heard the door open and close but
Elizete still held me tightly staring at the
latch. . . . Her man found us and I told her
that she had to come stay with me in town but
she said no. I stayed with her the night in case
he would come back and kill her. I don't know
what I thought I'd do. Shit. How many times
have I heard that this is what fucks up revolu-
tions? How the fuck am I going to get out of
it? She didn't talk to me all night, just touched
my face.

The Revolutionary Day celebrations were
overwhelming. The speech by the general of the
army was something else. I've never heard a
general with such a rapport with the people.
This was not an army standing on the wharf,
it was a people. I stood in the militia and the
love of the people all around us made me the
happiest I've been.

It just occurred to me how rough the last
months in Toronto were. I remember telling

Abena that I was coming for a rest. She didn't
understand and she warned me against coming
only to get a rest but today I feel well. It has
been a good opportunity to distance myself
and to collect myself. I've been reading a lot
and working hard. Thank God this Caribbean
is such a fucking mad place, too. Elizete's man
ran off and we haven't seen him since. She says
it's vindication. If I wasn't a materialist I'd
believe her. But I am, so I'm trying to persuade
her to come and stay with me. I can do so
much here even after working and talking all
day long. I read at night even when the electricity goes out. I have a lamp. I was really afraid
of losing parts of my memory but today I real-
ize that I'm healthy again. It rained for two
weeks and then this week the sky cleared up.
I've never seen such rain. Everything was
washed away, big gash in the earth where the
rain gouged it out. Things grow so fast I hardly
recognize some roads and paths any more.
Overgrown bushes and just green everywhere,
humid as hell.

I've lost my fountain pen. Two or three months
ago. I'll try to go to town and buy one tomorrow.

Well, this diary will not be a chronicle of anything that has happened. Sometimes I remember
to write in it, most times not. Elizete came to
stay with me.

Why am I so scared all the time? Even with
Elizete here. I was going to write about the revolution; instead this book is full of loneliness.
As soon as I think I'm all right it falls apart.
And nothing I can put my finger on, just some
small knowledge that it won't work out or if it
does I'll still be unhappy. No one is enough
company, no one enough absence.

The work is going well if slowly. By month's
end all of the strike planning will be done.
Surprisingly enough it was harder to convince
some of the younger workers. The old ones
were scared but they said they had nothing to
lose. By the end of the year we will turn the
plantation into a co-operative. It is no better
than a nineteenth-century *métayage*, if not worse.
One step short of slavery. I still think that
moving so slowly and trying to accommodate
these pigs only gives them time to undermine
the revo. They don't intend to give up a thing.

The land should have been taken away right
after the triumph but they didn't want to go so
fast, thinking that the middle class and the
owners would support the revolution since they
hated the former government too. As far as I'm
concerned the middle class can never be
trusted. Never.

A conflict has overtaken the central committee. I hope that they can fix it.

We're all waiting to see what happens to the
People's Revolutionary Government. Rumours
abound. The Caribbean is a forest of rumours.
It's how people get news. It's terribly distorted
and dangerous. Tomorrow I'm going to town,
to the market, to hear what the news vine says.
I've been here a year now. It seems shorter.

In the market eavesdropping on conversations,
the people are with Clive overwhelmingly. The
party must know this. Our militia meeting was
tense and some of the section leaders did not
attend. It's a complicated situation. I don't know
what I agree with. They've arrested Clive and
the militia is to stay on alert.

Overwhelming heat. Some rain. One p.m. Borrowed Elizete's umbrella to go to town to stretch my legs and see if I could pick up any news. I don't know how she can bear it. She's busy looking at okra plants and pumpkin vines and rain and talking about when to plant what and how dry this rainy season is. She has no idea. Not fair. I don't understand her. We're all hoping that this shit works out fast. In town a woman called to a man across the street, "They say you do wrong things, is true?" The man answered, "So they say." And the woman, "Is true nah." They're throwing words I know, the way word throwing is a way of challenge and safety. On the way back a comrade who works at the Tyre Mart hailed me. He came to the wall on my side and said he didn't feel good about what was going on and that the struggle wasn't the same, that he had heard that a militia unit had rebelled in Charlieville. He was so pained and worried. He looked at me and said, "You still firm on the question of democratic centralism?" He was mocking me, I knew. We had had many arguments before about party discipline, and I confess my position is weak if things are falling apart because of it. And how

can I say that comrades are overzealous in
Caicou if they're carrying out the instructions
of the central committee? The comrade said to
me if the people go one way and the party
another, the party is wrong no matter how
correct the political line. Then he said, "You
should know what I mean comrade." I had the
feeling that he was talking about Elizete and
me. It startled me a little and I didn't know
what to say. It's a small place.

In the middle of everything Elizete asks me
why I'm with her. Why I'm with her! This is
too much now. I don't want to be responsible
like that for anyone. I can't stand the feeling of
being attached. I'm trying to finish CLR.

I stayed home in the morning. Things were at
a standstill anyway. Yesterday I tried to get a
transport to the fields but it was like Sunday in
the market, empty. My head hurt this morning so
I lay down and Elizete brought me pumpkin seed
tea, or shining bush tea and God knows what.

About ten o'clock I heard shots. Through
the front window looking up the hill I saw

people up on the Mount Moriah Bridge. They
were chanting for Clive. I got up thinking that
I should report to my militia unit.

My head hurts like hell. Barometric pressure.
Rain. There's a curfew. It feels so personal
and...like being inside of a bleeding wound,
a gash. Clive is dead. I had so much hope for
this place. Rumours and rumours and justifica-
tions. The radio says that Clive and others
started the shooting and that they armed
civilians. Nobody believes them. Staying in
is getting on my nerves. We need milk,
bread, etc....

I am torn and afraid to say it, afraid to even
write it down. At first I thought that Clive was
wrong and I was even proud that we could
challenge the leader and have him submit to
the will of the party. Then it broke apart and
the outcome was not reason and discipline as I
expected. Then the people went to free Clive
from house arrest and I had to take it back. I
realized that at that moment the revolution
had triumphed because the people, people who
had been afraid, with all the governments

before, of expressing their will had come out and done just that, exactly what the revo said they could. I confess my analysis has deserted me. I want this thing to work so much whoever's left I'll follow.

Clive was a romantic. He needed great love to sweep him through actions. He was moved more by destiny than history. He waited for the people to come for him. When they did, that boy in his short pants was carried through the town and everyone was happy. Women talked about him like their child, men like their older brother. He knew his people well, better than the central committee and better than the army. He knew where they were in the street. When the school children and the people came and swept him up in their arms, he thought that their love, and his, was enough. The people had triumphed. If we could wipe out the last ten days we would be grateful.

People look to see how you bury their dead and if you grieve with their mothers. Soldiers are only loved by politicians. People love flesh and blood. They love who speaks to them.

There are no death announcements. They won't let people mourn Clive.

On the radio I hear that foreign troops are massing. The Americans and the other islands. They must love this. Shit. All of a sudden they love Clive. Now they're calling for isolation. Fuckers. How many people have they killed? Seven hundred in so-called democratic elections this year, police butchers on the young people in the National Union in the hills, thirty rastas killed in one year. The only thing they want to isolate and kill here is socialism. Fucking hypocrites.

Someone said that the function of a Third World country's army is not to repel invaders since it is probably so small and ill-equipped it could never match a superpower nor perhaps even a neighbour, but its function is to repress its people.

The BBC carried a nasty lie on Friday about looting and shots fired during the lifting of curfew. We went out to get pitch oil for the lamp, rice, matches and rum. The Americans

are sending a task force they say, fifteen ships,
an aircraft carrier to protect their citizens
here. Like hell. Their fucking citizens have the
best deal here. Who would touch them? Shit,
shit, shit.

My fucking head hurts so much. My body is
consuming me when I need it to run.

Each day of this I thought that it would end
the very next minute. It did not occur to me
that it would continue. Talk about naive. I am
such an ass. Why can't I figure it out? Every
minute tumbles on the other.

The radio keeps saying to report to the section. They say Choiselle reported and Grenade.
The comrades in Choiselle worked round the
clock for weeks building the sea wall. I guess
I'll go today.

Today I feel calm but I don't want anyone to
touch me and I'm not turning the radio on. I'm
not leaving this place. I'm not moving.

Five o'clock in the morning I heard the droning

of their planes in the sky. I am so angry I
will break.

The radio is playing up-tempo music as if
nothing is happening. I can't stand it. I wish
Elizete would turn the fucking thing off. I've
got to get out of here. If I don't my head will
split in many, many pieces.

I'm putting my clothes on. The radio went
off. I'm going to meet the other cadres. My
head is hurting me.

Elizete, she, arrived again at Abena's hands, her thumbs chasing each other, her fingers fused. Yes, this was the kind of woman Verlia would have been. Sitting in an office on Vaughan Road counselling, "Go home, it's not a place for us." After thirteen winters, she would not see who was in front of her any more; she'd sat there, hearing the stories, saying do this, do that, saying at first it was possible and you had a right to come. Then as the fatality of it crawled into her, this might have come out of her fast and as surprising, "Go home, this is not a place for us." Well, as if anybody thought so. As if anybody would dream. Everybody knew it was temporary. This was a place to make money, someone had said to her, not a place to live. What money could be made. None if your skin was Black and nothing hanging between your legs. Oh, you could scrimp, take any damn thing they had to offer and hear them bad-talk your colour. But you couldn't live. And you were just one in a crowd, honey.

And Abena, reading Elizete's face and not answering her

could only say this now, long after Verlia could say I told you, long since Verlia was gone and waiting for Elizete to arrive, she could say it like she was heading home herself, something that was unsaid but always hovering, waiting to be said and heard: "Go home, this is not a place for us." Go home, it's not a place for the soul, you'll end up damaged, you'll end up blind, you'll end up not knowing, hell, not liking who you are. She'd had it all, seen it all. Now she wasn't sure who the hatred was for. The women who kept coming or the thing that hurt them. Yes, she'd seen them. She was their sister and their daughter. She'd been a daughter. Arrived here as a daughter at twelve to meet her mother. These women, our mothers, a whole generation of them, left us. They went to England or America or Canada or some big city as fast as their wit could get them there because they were women and all they had to live on was wit since nobody considered them whole people. They scraped money together, pawned jewellery, sewed *peau de soir* and *guipure* lace to well-off women's bodies, squeezing out a yard on the side, made *pacotille* in rooms with their children sleeping or quarrelled with their fathers about men to marry them or left their girl child with their boyfriends at night while they sold roast corn on highways unsuspecting. They put it away coin by coin, wrinkled dollar by wrinkled dollar, stuffed it in mattresses or in brassières or tied in the corners of petticoats until it swelled to the ticket of their dreams, the boat or the plane that would empty them on another continent where they could join life as they were sure they were not living. They sent for us, sent for us daughters, then washed our faces in their self-hatred. Self-hatred they had learned from the white people whose toilets they had cleaned, whose asses they had wiped, whose kitchens they had scrubbed, whose hatred they had swallowed, and when they sent for us, they hated us because they saw their reflection in us, they saw their hands swollen with water, muscular with lifting and pulling, they saw their souls assaulted and irrecoverable, wounded from insult and the sheer nastiness of white words and they beat us abused us terrorized us as they had been terrorized and beaten and abused; they saw nothing good in us because they saw nothing good in themselves. They made us pay for what they had suffered. Yes, she had been a daughter. They did not feel redeemed by it but they themselves had been so twisted from walking in shame that they twisted our bodies to suit their stride. They said, "Oh, you think you're better than your mother" even when they swore with each blow that they wanted us to be better. They could not bear nor satisfy our hopefulness. All the news we received of them, all the news they sent, hopefulness, we carried in book bags and patent-leather shoes from away. So they tried to stanch it like bleeding. We bled on their hands, they cut our backs open, they closed their eyes to us. All they gave us was self-hatred. They called us "nigger" like any white man would, because when they spilled out on this other continent they understood the first time a white voice spoke to them that they were less than they thought. These women, walking the streets of any city, their bodies, girdled and braced, restraining what they have forgotten, like joy or sweets sugaring in their hands many years ago for a girl child, now could not look at us without wincing, sweating in their palms. She had been a daughter. Yes, go on home, this is not a place for us. Go watch your girl child rip her dress on fences she's trying to scale and catch her talking to herself counting cracks in the road and, even if you have nothing to eat, it will be better than this death to obscurity and mean spiritedness.

She wanted to undo Abena's fist, smooth it out into a hand. She had come here to give help or to get help and had got some kind of wisdom she didn't need and couldn't use. Mean, well there wasn't a place that she had been that.... She just wanted a place to sit down to sort her head out. Was there no place like that? Jesus. Now here was this one with her body balled up in a fist and the only thought coming to her was more names for Adela. Close up and frighten vine, bitter bark water, one minute rain, gully wash away rain, ever everlasting rain, speckled throat fowl, I alone bird. This woman must think she was mad, staring at her, muttering these names. Well, two of us mad then, sister. She had not even spoken to her, had not even asked her what she wanted, just assumed at first that she was pregnant and illegal as all the women who came to her. She only needed a place to sort her head out. Pregnant all right. Call it that then. Full of all the things that had happened to her... tremble tremble leaf, big head batchac, edge teeth fruit, falling down road, kitty corner tree.... Anybody could see that she was illegal she thought and she supposed the other went along with it. Pregnant and illegal. One thing followed the other. Trying to be legal you became pregnant and even more illegal. One way or the other, a woman was always pregnant. Drink castor oil, eat green guava, sit over a hot pot of water, mustard plaster... One way or the other, full of something. A few days, she needed a few days to sort it out. Why she'd come here. Well this one with the tight fist said it was okay. So she'd lay down here. She'd lay right down here. Right here. Fine if she didn't recognize her and was too busy to see who she was. Go home my ass anyway. She think anything simple like that? She'd just stop here for a bit. Watch her hard in the face see if it made a difference. She was tired. Tired anyway. The room was full of paper tumbling, tumbling off the desk. She would make a bed under the window. Clean the room a bit. It would be nice to wake up under the window. Right there under the window was fine.

The fist said she would let her sleep in the morning up to ten, it would be Saturday but she had to work there anyway, she worked every day, lots to do. She heard her; it seemed no sooner had she closed her eyes, she'd slipped into the room, watched Elizete under the window sleeping and sat for awhile watching. Turning in her sleep Elizete felt her close to her face saying, "I came when I was twelve you know. My mother sent for me. But I wasn't what she wanted and she wasn't what I imagined. We were both disappointed. I couldn't speak I was so unhappy. She thought that I was stubborn and wilful. So she began hitting me. The more she hit the less I said. I couldn't help it, I was stunned."

Sleep was tight in her eyes, the woman had returned. It was only seven and dark was not over but she had returned to finish talking, as she had left, as if she had left in the middle. What time was it? Was it morning? And how many days had she been in this country, where was it? The woman wanted to know how many days, how long, who had told her to come here. Behind her eyelids she heard the rat-a-tat-tat of her questions. She was sure it didn't matter. It had only been somewhere Verlia mentioned, the place where perhaps she could see something of her. She wanted to wake up this morning under the window. She had placed the bedding just so to look at the wood of the desk so it wasn't the desk, and the window so it wasn't this window, when she woke up. She did it instinctively, to centre herself, to wake up as she had done thinking of Adela, thinking of her tasks each day of getting water, weeding the provisions that needed weeding and leaving the weeds for medicine, of driving goats from the weeds, fanning flies from the meat, walking far. She did it instinctively making up names that would soothe her. And names that would take her to the walls of the house where she'd started her catalogue of names for Adela. She did not expect change any more, only reversion. She knew that she would exist, unfortunately or for ever, if she lay underneath a window or if she came peering into the face of a woman at a kitchen door or if she had the urge to open a woman's fists or even if she saw a woman sweating in a field. Urge, limber and lengthy, conquered her physical being. Urge conquered her voice and her hands and her thoughts and her straying. Perhaps she could collect herself lying under a window, wood in her vision. Come close weed, my dear plant, quaily skin bean, snake vine, dead man fingers, jump up and kiss me flower, candle wax lily. And after the first moment she didn't care anyway if the woman did not know that it was she, Elizete, lover to Verlia who was lover to her. What did it matter anyway, she had only wanted to see her to see what Verlia meant by "not enough", to measure if she was not enough too and if that was why Verlia left her, lying on stones.

In the daytime she went back to her room in the second place with Jocelyn, but in the night she was restless so she came back here. In and out and more and more like someone who did not know if they were coming out or going in until she lay under the window.

Each morning on mornings since she'd been here, the woman would come in early, after promising to leave her alone to sleep. She'd come in, expectantly, talking though she didn't seem to need any reply. Just began. Sitting at the desk playing with the papers Elizete had fixed the night before, piling them back on the desk, doing something with her hands, trying not to ball them into fists. Earlier and earlier until it seemed she didn't leave at night at all, begging Elizete to open her eyes, stay with her. Listen.

"I often wondered what my mother was beating me into. What the hell were you making, I hear a conversation with her in my head ask years later. What did she see becoming under her hand? Was it an icon, akuaba eyes where her hand descended like a machete, so angular, so severe. And this jowly sullenness — did she see herself kneading and kneading and leaving it to rise or did she want something more stiff, more assuming cold brass or the stillness of iron? But I know that if I received all her blows, if I interpreted her intention right, I would be the ugliest woman on earth. If she intended to make a shape and if somehow I as her subject acknowledged her movement, gave in to her impressions, her thoughts, her artistic decisions, if she were somehow an artist, then I would be a ruin or less fabulous, put aside, hardly recognizable as human."

Was her voice easing or was it that she was talking to herself, hearing it in her head, playing with the sound of herself until only the sound itself mattered, how perfect it was, how truthful it was and she had arrived at it. She seemed to reach the end that morning and Elizete lying under the window murmuring her names did not stop but gave her the music to finish. Blue fly, bottle fish, butter nose, sugar head, ant road, sandy house. Elizete did not stop though she thought that she heard weeping but Abena was dry-eyed and shining as if she'd finally understood, she'd finally put it in words and understood not her mother whom she'd always understood as a piece of science even when she could only watch her and say nothing. She simply could not fathom her mother not seeing what she saw. How she saw her mother, in the middle of her life, all foolish and preten-tious and wanting what white people had, which was like wanting us all dead. This is what she wanted to explain to her mother in that look she gave her, that look which her mother thought was impudence and stubbornness. That look which still lasts when she meets her. That look that still confronts her mother's talk about how she is wasting herself, how she could have been so much, she could have made so much money and why does she waste her time with no good people, people who will bring you down. That look she takes with her out the door and it doesn't go away for days. And it has to be months before she can see her again. Weeks before she can call. Now her mother lives as most mothers live, in highrises smelling of the plastic on their couches. They live alone among their collections of small silver spoons or doilies or cups or dolls, their feet swollen, their minds turned to evangelism. No child visits them out of love, just out of pity.

She let it go, making her words float into perfection, slipping off her tongue so sane. "Let it go, let it go, let it go." She knows that it has harmed her, so many chances she hasn't taken, so many moves she hasn't made. It has stiffened her. She could have gone with Vee, but she'd been paralysed. When Vee said, "I have to go, Abena." She'd lain still, paralysed, her arms still in the shape of Vee, and she'd fallen asleep, for her fear, while Vee got up, paced around and then left the apartment. If someone wanted an emotion from her it paralysed her. Stopped her dead. It was like looking through glass. Emotions were too dramatic for her. If someone asked her for one she only gazed at them sliding as far back in her head as she could. Recoiled. Repelled. Then as if waking up the opportunity would be gone. She could not act quickly or decisively in any situation that involved her. For other people maybe but not for herself. For herself she turned to glass. She suddenly felt as if she could not move. The only thing she'd done on her own behalf was change her name and that was long before she met Vee. In a moment of relief from the stiffness in her soul. From June to Abena.

She'd thought that it might be the beginning of her changing. Ridding herself of the name her mother had given her. How she would not have to hear that name called, pouring out hopelessness. And it was the beginning of change but it was more difficult than she imagined. It was harder to change how she had been made inside. Emotions. She'd cut them off to stave off her mother's blows. She could not find them when someone, not someone with a belt or a stick, but someone who liked her genuinely, when someone like that asked her for them. She could not find them. She thought that they were asking for something else. Asking for her failure or her fear. Then she turned to glass. She heard them rip and tear when she was called to give them. She could not pull them out of herself. She depended on others to read them for her and then she nodded yes and no. She liked to fix others, show them what they couldn't see and what they might do so she stayed and worked in this office. She had a good view of the insides of others. Before they hit the door she could read their need, their want and what would make them better.

And when Vee got back to the apartment she was so afraid she still lay there stiffly and said nothing. Though she wanted to say, "I'll come, too," and she wanted to say "Don't leave, Vee." But she said nothing and talk was hard between them because Vee didn't give any room, not another word of offer or encouragement. Vee's face was sealed and determined.

She was holding her own self together, trying to save her own life, Abena knew but could not break her own voice open to say, "I'll come, Vee," "Don't go, Vee." The last month was hell. They walked around each other and talked around each other and tried not to be in the apartment together and she never met Vee's look. All the while she was hoping that at the last minute it would come out of her and Vee would see it, hear her saying, "Vee, please, please, please do it for me, stay, just this once. I promise I'll try harder." At the last minute Vee might change her mind, turn around and see how much she wanted her to stay. Nothing like that happened and Vee left and she stayed and shrunk herself into two tight humid fists.

Vee's mind was on her own life and anybody coming with her would have to know that and have to want to save themselves too. She didn't want to save anyone else from this country. Too fast now. Abena still had to figure out the shape of her face, she still felt the machete blade against her cheek-bone, she still visited her mother and said nothing through her berating, she looked into the well of her face, to see behind her words and saw nothing and this so fascinated and frightened her she did not say, "Vee, I'll come." Vee couldn't wait on anyone drowning in the face of her mother. Vee didn't want to be pulled in with her. Vee.

"You wasn't enough and I wasn't there." Elizete under the window in the first words Abena allowed herself to hear, seeing as how she was finished and realized that she had not heard anything from this woman and had only allowed that she was a woman needing help who at this moment she couldn't help because she needed help herself. And refusing to hear her because she didn't want to hear about Verlia yet. She heard it on the news and her head had spun with not wanting to know and then she didn't hear and she knew. Now she was finished and it was like knowing. She needed a woman lying under a window half out of her mind who could appreciate it. And all that murmuring filled in the spaces that her own murmuring left. It was soothing to be understood. The first time she heard her murmuring in between her saying "go home," she knew that what she herself had to tell would fit well in the middle of this noise. She knew that it had a place in between names and grass and murmuring. That way it would go. She stooped to the floor putting her face against Elizete's. She lay there too, looking at the window and the wood.

"Not enough? She said that?"

"Not enough."

"I know. I wanted her to wait."

"Wait? For what?"

"What about you?"

"She jump. Leap from me. Then I decide to count the endless name of stones. Rock leap, wall heart, rip eye, cease breath, marl cut, blood leap, clay deep, coal dead, coal deep, never rot, never cease, sand high, bone dirt, dust hard, mud bird, mud fish, mud word, rock flower, coral water, coral heart, coral breath..."

One dreamed she multiplied into pieces and flew away, one dreamed his feet clawed and he flew away, one dreamed she feathered and flew away, one dreamed he sprang like a tree, one dreamed she blew into dust, one dreamed her dress dried into a stone, one dreamed he shrank from sight little by little, one dreamed his arms took flight, one dreamed his mouth beaked, one dreamed light, one dreamed light, light, one dreamed light made her fly, one dreamed lifting a baby, one dreamed eating snow cones, one dreamed eating pepper, one dreamed pounding cassava, one dreamed blowing farine, one dreamed cutting cake, one dreamed a year backwards, one dreamed a year forward, one dreamed of rocking. All dreamed and dreamed. All dreamed and dreamed and dreamed they flew away. The one in the red, his head alone flying, and the one in the green, her head aching, stayed awake dreaming. The ones in black screamed.

"I'm not dying in this fucking cemetery!"

Verlia, screaming, screaming through the gathering of dreams, the aerie of dreams at the tombstones.

"I'm awake. I'm staying awake."

She is awake to the grit, grit, groaning bombs' groan. She is awake. She is awake to the fire in her skin. She wanted to rip her uniform off because of the burning, her body on fire without flames. Her skin thaws of the deadening sleep, it thaws to burning. Fire. Her body is on fire. Her uniform is like flame.

"Comrades, comrades, comrades, let's go. I'm not dying in this fucking cemetery today."

She woke them up to the fire in their own bodies, the dreaminess of dying in the cemetery, of sweet claws and sweet wings and sweet beaks and multiplying. She woke them up to fire. Her uniform was wet with sweat, but her skin burned, burned like oil and coals and paper. She found her legs, thinner and shakier than when she'd first knelt down at the tombstone. Not dying in this fucking cemetery, not sleeping, not sleeping, not sleeping. The terrible brightness of the sun at one o'clock. Its coal-white burn, its lashing, lashing the middle of the head. Not today, not today, not today. Her skin itchy, itchy with flame. Her belly stiff and bursting with flames. Not today, not today.

"Let's go, let's go comrades, let's go," to the boy in the red bandanna's, "MIGs, MIGs, MIGs."

"Not sleeping, not fucking sleeping," to the red bandanna spinning MIGs, MIGs, to the *grn, grn, grn grnnn* of the sky.

They ran out of the awful brightness of the cemetery, they ran out of their dreams, her head saying not today, not today, not today, round Circular Street up the fort road. They were heading for the fort, the comfort of the stone walls, the height, the lovely view of the sea and the harbour. She did all that she could with her body, pushed and pushed her legs to the walls, gave her flesh to running and running. Her body watering and emptying, her breathing so fast for her breath it burned. Her eyes unblinking. She could see the calm of the ocean, her heart so big she heard it in her ear. And pushing and running and running and forgetting she felt someone behind her, "Comrade, run! Comrade, sister, lover, run, not today, not today." Up the fort road, the steep, steep, gravel road, clothes heavy, heavy wet, the dry season sky, the dry dry day, the bees barking, the cicada shouts, heat waving through her rain of sweat. Who was behind her. Who was she leaving. "Run, comrade!"

Lost her when they got to the fort, to the cliff overlooking the sea, spinning around, all of them now, firing in the air now like the boy in the red bandanna screaming. In the bullets at their back, sudden and surprised like flocks of birds flying, shooting into the sky. The noise like the world cracking. She hit the ground, tunnelling dust, rolling the yellow-white rock face, gravel in her mouth, and dust, her body, solid, her whole weight resting on her chest, hitting the ground, solid. When she thought about it, solid as usual, its usual weight hitting something solid, ground. And think-ing, Elizete turned her head to remark it to Verlia, to smile about how she always hit solid ground, and turned her head to say it but saw Verlia, running, turning, leap off the cliff. Her green, green wet clothing flattened to her, her back leap, her face awake, all of her soar, her arms out wide, her chest pulling air, leap. Green, green. Verlia leaping.

Someone taking a shot of rum across the harbour saw them fall, saw the arms out wide at the end of the cliff, heard the pound, pound, pound *po, po, po, po, pound* of the guns driving them off the cliff's side into the sea. Someone saw the steel black shank of the armoured cars crumbling the cliff top. Someone who could not stop shaking. Some-one spilling rum saw them tumble, hit, break their necks, legs, spines, down the cliff side and some of them flew, leapt into the ocean. Someone saw the embrace. A long and dead arc, green and black hitting turquoise.

She is laughing and laughing and laughing. It actually happened, that the water is emerald and choppy and the house is going off to sea, that the waves have swept the house away leaving the bleached pillow trees like excla-mation points in the sand. She's flying out to sea and in the emerald she sees the sea, its eyes translucent, its back solid going to some place so old there's no memory of it. She's leaping. She's tasting her own tears and she is weightless and deadly. She feels nothing except the bubble of a laugh each time she breathes. Her body is cool, cool in the air. Her body has fallen away, is just a line, an electric current, the sign of lightning left after lightning, a faultless arc to the deep turquoise deep. She doesn't need air. She's in some other place already, less tortuous, less fleshy.

ACKNOWLEDGEMENTS

My gratitude to Faith Nolan, Leleti Tamu, Filomena Carvalho, Ted Chamberlin, Adrienne Rich, Claire Harris and Patricia Murphy for their patience, encouragement, criticism, constant reading and generous friendship.

The first quotation on page 157 is from The Last Poets recording of the poem "On The Subway" (New York: Douglas 3 East Wind Association, 1970. Distributed by Pip Records). The second quotation on that page is from Frantz Fanon's book *The Wretched of the Earth* (New York: Grove/Atlantic, Inc., 1963). Used by permission. I quote from it again on page 159. Quotations on page 160 are from two poems by Nikki Giovanni, "Poem for Aretha" and "For Saundra", published in *The Black Poets, A New Anthology*, edited by Dudley Randall (New York: Bantam Books, 1971). Ernesto Che Guevara's "Letter to Carlos Quejana" quoted on pages 165 and 183 appeared in *Socialism and Man in Cuba* by Che Guevara and Fidel Castro (New York: Pathfinder, 1989).

I wish to thank the Ontario Arts Council for a Works-in-Progress grant that assisted in the completion of this novel.

— D.B.